The Dragon from Guǎngzhōu

To Raymond. Thanks for all the love and support.

Copyright © D.W. Plato 2021

This manuscript is meant for entertainment purposes only.

Any resemblance to real persons, living or dead, is purely coincidental.

No part of this book shall be copied or reproduced without explicit

permission from the author.

Edited by Kimberly Hunt, Revision Division, Baltimore, Maryland, U.S.A

Cover art design by Jayden Weist, Hamburg, Germany

1801 - Off the shore of Guǎngzhōu, South China

<u>Chapter One – A Girl Named Mógū</u>

The stiff leather hood had been cinched firm around her neck. Danger danced on her flesh. She felt the fumbling of the knot being undone below her chin. The fear thick in her throat caused her heart rate to flare. Who were these people who had kidnapped her?

Fresh air, tinged with incense, filled her nostrils as the hood was pulled off. Mógū (Mushroom) breathed deep. Her eyes were already adjusted to the dark. Candles flickered and danced creating a warm comforting atmosphere. A bedchamber?

Large, colorful silk pillows were piled high on an oversized bed. Ornate wood carvings adorned each piece of furniture. Everything she saw screamed wealth. The furnishings were luxurious, the art on the walls, even the rug under her bare feet was plush and expensive. From the corner of her eye, she saw a figure sitting at a little table at the far end of the room. She squinted in the dim light trying to make out facial features. The man rose and leisurely moved into her line of vision.

"It was you?" she questioned as recognition settled. Her face knotted in confusion and she felt as if she may get sick. The incense suddenly seemed to choke her as the memories of the day before crashed into her thoughts, the carnage on the flower boat, the terror, the blood. Chūntáo. She shook her head blocking the images still fresh in her mind.

The man smiled with confidence and reached out to stroke her cheek. His voice was calm, "Hello, my dear."

Twelve hours earlier ~

Shrill screams, high pitched and pained, startled Mógū. It was dawn and the young woman had been looking forward to getting some sleep. She had taken most of her work garb off and stood stock-still in her undergarments. Her twelve-hour shift on the floating brothel ended when the sun came up. It would start again at dusk. She preferred being available to their clients at night; evening trysts were much more fun and often included booze and opium. Another shriek from a different location on the upper deck sent a shiver down her spine.

Moving with the stealth and quickness of a cat, she retrieved her ten-inch dagger and, for good measure, took the broom handle she used to blockade her door in her other hand. Silently, she tip-toed into the hallway of the flower boat, all of her senses on high alert.

As Mógū crept up the narrow treads to the upper deck she heard the unmistakable grunts of a man engaged in intercourse. There was also a muffled, thin mewling of a woman in pain. Sunlight blinded her momentarily.

Sex was expected on the flower boat, it was a floating whorehouse after all, but what she saw was surprising. One of the prostitutes was being accosted against her will. The man had the woman pinned to the wooden planks of the deck. He had her head bent to one side while covering her mouth with his beefy hand. Her feet kicked and she twisted under his heft. Mógū noticed the woman's lotus feet and knew which of the young women it was. Fury flared in her chest.

Without thinking she stuck her dagger with force into the tender fold of the man's buttock and withdrew it quickly. He gave a sharp yip then moved from the woman, confused and pained. His and Mógū's gaze met. Fast and with force, she plunged the dagger deep into his neck, twisted it and pulled it out. Blood squirted at an odd angle, up and out. Pale-faced, he staggered towards her in a last attempt to do her harm. She brought the broom handle down on the back of his skull. *Crack!* The noise was sickening and satisfying at the same time. The young, weeping woman crawled to the stairwell and disappeared.

It took Mógū only a moment to realize their boat was under attack. *Who would do such a thing?* she wondered on the run. Prostitution was illegal in Guǎngzhōu but the government had made an exception for the flower boats since officially they were in the harbor. All the men who visited loved the service and attention the flower boats offered. Many came back time and time again. Most government officials made regular visits. They all treasured the flower boats from professionals to laymen.

This attack didn't make any sense. They were just a bunch of women working to make ends meet. Mógū had to find her best friend, Chūntáo (Spring Peach). She knew her lifelong pal wouldn't protect or defend herself. *Where could she be?*

Mógū raced to the kitchen on impulse. Sure enough, Chūntáo was there huddled behind a barrel of rice. Her eyes were wider than normal, and her face was completely drained of color. Relief overcame Mógū as she approached. The two of them had been through so much together. Chūntáo was the only family she had; their bond was as strong as steel.

"What's happening?" she sniveled as she stood.

Mógū shrugged and offered her friend a comforting smile.

"Why would you think I would know?"

"You like turmoil, admit it," Chūntáo mocked and moved towards her friend.

"No, I don't," Mógū said, a little perturbed.

Suddenly, one of the attackers stepped from the doorway. He drove his sword blade through Chūntáo's back. It tore through her gown and poked out of her chest. Her round face froze in an expression of surprise as she fell forward off the man's blade.

"NO!" Mógū screamed. The man swung his sword at her but she was quicker. She ducked under the deadly swipe. Crouched down, she ran towards her assailant. She rammed the top of her head into the man's groin full force. The bellow from him let her know she hit the mark. Mógū scooped up his dropped weapon. In one fluid motion, she stood and beheaded him. The razor-sharp sword hesitated only slightly as it went through his spine. She heard a dull thunk when his skull hit the deck. The body fell a moment after.

Mógū turned her attention to Chūntáo. Blood oozed through the front of her garments. She was trembling and very pale.

"No, no, no," Mógū chanted and knelt beside her wounded friend.

"This is not good," Chūntáo whispered, "not good at all."

"Sshhh, it'll be alright," Mógū answered with more confidence than she felt.

"Easy for you to say, you're not hemorrhaging—"

"Be quiet," Mógū said with authority, "seriously, shh…"

With force, she tore the woman's bodice open. She made two strips of fabric with the front and with delicacy, she cinched it tight to stop the bleeding.

"Can you breathe?" she asked. Chūntáo's eyes were closed but she nodded. The color had completely drained from the young woman's face; her lips had turned a light shade of blue.

Mógū glanced between Chūntáo and the melee. Panic washed over her as a sickening feeling settled into her gut. *Why? Who? How?* So many questions tumbled through her mind as she tried to piece together the scene taking place around her.

A lithe figure caught Mógū's attention. A painted face in a traditional white, black and red concubine style smiled at her. The figure moved with fluidity, swaying as if it were dancing. Confusion disarmed her brain. How had she not met this woman before? Was she a call girl? A new addition to the flower boat? Or part of the raid? Concubines raiding a brothel boat? None of this made sense.

Their eyes were locked as Mógū stood and studied the pretty face. She found herself returning a slight smile a split second before the black leather hood appeared from the folds of the woman's dress and descended over her face.

Mógū fought and struggled. She clawed at her captor's arms. This was man strength she realized with a sense of hopelessness, as she felt the rope being securely fastened around her neck. Like a sack of potatoes, she was heaved over the shoulder of her abductor and carried off the burning boat.

Although it had only been hours, it seemed like days before the dreadful hood was taken off her face.

"Hello, my dear," Zhèng Yī said to her as he gently stroked her cheek.

Chapter Two – Love is Overrated

Mógū lay in the bed replaying the day's events in her head. Zhèng Yī's proposal was bizarre. Last night she had been expecting him, he was a regular. Her favorite regular. They had a relationship that went beyond the bed. She would have called Zhèng Yī a friend or at the least, a business partner. Over the years, he had given her plenty of extra money to whisper information from some of her other powerful clients. It had become a game to her, a well-paid and well-played game.

When the government official, Gen Gui, visited her chamber, she played the simple girl he desired. Being a successful mole came with a certain amount of acting. It's what her bed-romping escapades had turned into, a charade where she became who the paying patron craved. This tactic had created quite a reputation. Mógū was the busiest and best paid whore on the flower boat.

With Gui she asked simple questions about what he did and then pumped his frail male ego.

"You chase pirates?" she asked him, looking up through her makeup-caked lashes. She would take her clothes off and sit on his lap naked. "Aren't you scared?" she would coo as her hips began to rotate on Gui's lap and she would feel his manhood grow under her bottom.

"You've got to think like a pirate and stay one step ahead of them," Gui said as he lifted her from him, and undid his pants, but he always kept talking. "To be a successful law enforcer, one must have some streak of being a criminal."

"So true, so smart." She would usually encourage the conversation with flattery. "So brave."

Mógū smiled and thought of the other men in power she had gotten lip-locked information from. She knew the intelligence wasn't all for Zhèng Yī but his family too, specifically his brother, Zhèng Sì. The Zhèng family were the most notorious pirates of the South Seas and the most powerful family she knew. It seemed everyone knew the Zhèng brothers and their villainous father, if they didn't know them personally, they knew of them.

Little brother, Zhèng Sì, had been a customer on the flower boat too. She noted she had never had sex with him and wondered which girl he had preferred. She pondered whether Zhèng Yī had laid claim to her and perhaps that's why Zhèng Sì had never requested her bed specifically.

A light rap on the door brought Mógū back to the present. The slender young woman she now recognized from the flower boat seemed to float in and settled herself on a chair opposite Mógū. She tinkered with something she held in her long, slender fingers. Mógū kept her eyes on the woman's perfectly painted face as she continued to turn it over and over.

The woman stopped playing with the object and set it on the little table next to her. Mógū now recognized what it was, the tiny doll of her likeness from the brothel boat. Each working woman had one of these little dolls fashioned to resemble her. The madam would lay the dolls down while the girls were with a client. If the doll stood, the woman was available for an appointment. With Mógū, her doll rarely, if ever, stood. Sometimes, the madam would place flat green soy beans in front of Mógū's doll as the men would line up to be with her and each bean represented the next patron.

On average, Mógū would service four men an hour. In her mind, she approached each man as a business exchange. Most times, she would come across forceful, in charge. Powerful men seemed to like domination. Often, fifteen minutes was too long. The nights that Zhèng Yī visited were her favorite. He would pay for the remainder of her shift and they would indulge in the fine opium and rum he brought. She would tell him the secrets she got from her powerful, government connected clients and he would trade them for the bitter, tar-like substance she loved to smoke. She turned her attention to her caller, barring the memories.

"Isn't it time you thought about a career where you can stand on your own two feet instead of working from between your legs?" The voice was low, smoky and direct. Mógū's eyes flickered to the little doll standing on the bedside table.

"I'm not going to be second wife," she said defiantly.

"Of course not," the visitor cooed, "first wife."

Mógū's face knitted into confusion. "Who are you?"

"Cheung Po Tsai of Shenyáng. Lovely to make your acquaintance," A warm, sexy smile accompanied the introduction.

Something wasn't right. "Cheung Po Tsai?" Mógū's eyes dropped to the woman's feet. "Shenyáng?" The visitor's feet slid under the chair and allowed the long dress to cover them. "When I saw you on the flower boat, you certainly didn't appear like a proper lady from Shenyáng." Mógū knew high ranked women from that area would certainly have bound feet.

"You're a clever girl," Cheung Po Tsai said. "You got me, I'm not really from Shenyáng—"

"And you're not really a woman," Mógū guessed remembering the strength of her abductor. Their eyes met and she knew the truth of this person's gender. "I would have just come with you," Mógū continued, "why did you have to kill Chūntáo?"

Cheung Po Tsai coyly dipped his head. "I didn't kill your friend," he said feigning innocence, "you know what they say, boys will be—"

"Stop!" Mógū interrupted, she shook her head and lay back on the bed, "What do you want from me?"

"Zhèng Yī was pretty clear with his proposal, was he not?"

Her mind drifted to Zhèng Yī's proposal, the way he had knelt in front of her and extended his hand, presenting the emerald ring. Her face flushed as she recalled her sharp words, *Why would I marry you?* She hadn't meant it to come out so rough, but it was a legitimate question. Zhèng Yī was a notorious criminal. He had laughed at her and told her to sleep on it then left the chamber. The memory caused a wave of heat across her neck and up to her ears.

"I don't love him," was all she could mutter. She hadn't slept in over twenty-four hours and the deprivation was taking hold. She could use some shuteye.

"Love is overrated," Cheung Po Tsai replied. "Think of the doors his family's name could open for you..." he continued to prattle on, citing facts about Zhèng Yī's family she already knew, everything he was blathering on about was common knowledge.

"First wife, huh?" she said more to herself.

She sat back up and stared at Po Tsai who looked injured after being interrupted. Perhaps it was the lack of sleep or a combination with the surreal situation but her mind started snapping. Good fortune and luck were smiling down at her at the same time and she needed to be smart enough to recognize the opportunity. Thanks to the suggestion of her kidnapper, the possibilities of marrying into this notorious family loomed more like a career path than a husband-wife relationship.

Her mind flashed back to the night before. The conversation should have been her first clue about her potential future.

"It's rare to find a woman like you," Zhèng Yī had said and played his card. The game was madí'ào, the object was to collect groups of symbols to score points and discard the ones that didn't match. Some nights, she and Zhèng Yī played into the early morning hours.

Mógū turned the card of the 'banker' and laid her winning card.

"A woman like me?" she asked, scooping up the cards and dealing out the next hand.

"A woman of quiet power." His voice had turned silky. "Brains and beauty, a rare combination."

"Thank you, but I'm not really the marrying type," she answered while she studied her recently dealt cards, "can't cook and I don't want children." She smiled at him as she laid down her first card.

Mógū shook her head to stop the memory from going further as she studied Cheung Po Tsai. Oddly, she began to picture him without his makeup, without the hair pinned up in a bamboo stick but instead braided down his back like a traditional warrior. He was handsome in a beautiful feminine way. Her eyes dropped to his hands which were folded in his lap like a proper lady. She thought about those hands touching her. Were they soft like a woman's or rough like a working man's hands?

"Oh, I almost forgot," Po Tsai said with exuberance, his smile crooked, eyes bright, "I need a mommy."

Mógū's momentary fantasy halted. "Mommy?"

"To become a legal heir, I must become Zhèng Yī's son," Po Tsai's smile was disarming. "To be adopted, there needs to be parents. Plural. Zhèng Yī didn't mention that?" Her face was twisted into puzzlement. "He needs to be married...Mom," Po Tsai winked.

Mógū noticed the definite shape of the bob in his throat only men had. How had she missed it before? He pulled the bamboo from his hair. The heavy black mane cascaded down over his shoulders. He was truly a lovely man.

Mógū nodded. "A wife and a mother all wrapped up in one tidy package."

"Yeah," he said, "that's definitely one way to look at it."

They looked at each other and she saw the seriousness of the conversation peeking out from behind his smiling eyes. Something about the way he looked now with the makeup smeared and his hair disarrayed caused the images of the previous morning to ping through her head. The last image was of Chūntáo. Grief knotted in her heart. "If you came to the flower boat for me, why did you kill the other girls?"

Po Tsai shrugged, "I didn't kill anyone yesterday," he protested and held his hands up in a surrender gesture. "The men do what they do, I have no control over them. They get a little zealous, that's all. They certainly weren't instructed to kill helpless women, but there may have been a causality or two. It comes with the occupation."

Mógū looked away and shook her head, tears stung her eyes but she wouldn't let Po Tsai see any emotion from her. Gurgle noises bubbled from her stomach. Po Tsai smiled and handed her a mini-sized sandwich with chicken and cabbage from a tray that sat near the door. She accepted gratefully and bit into it as he poured the tea. It was over-steeped and cold.

"Tell Zhèng Yī I'll consider," she said and watched his expression.

"You'll consider?" He laughed, his answer coming a bit too quick. "How much longer would you really live prosperously on the flower boats?" He gave her a hard look up and down. "Quit while you're ahead."

She rolled her eyes then spoke, "You don't know anything about me or my career choice."

"I'd bet my last booty your career choice wasn't yours," he took another bite of the sandwich.

She shrugged, knowing he was right. A few moments of silence passed between them.

Mógū broke the silence. "I want half."

"Half of what?"

"The treasure, the fleet, the land, all of it," she deadpanned.

Po Tsai laughed. "I'm not sure we need a woman in our lives *that* bad."

"I'm serious," she said and took another sandwich from the tray. "I may even consider bearing him a son." She took a bite and spoke through the food, "I don't believe that is something you can offer him."

"Oh, this is how it's going to be? There are three of us, that cuts my fortune to a third!"

"Oh, this is how it's going to be," she mocked him and continued, "One of us will die before the other two, those are the odds, the facts of life. If it's me, you're back to half. If it's Zhèng Yī, you're back to half." She sighed heavily and spoke as if to a small child. "If it's you, it doesn't matter, you'll be dead," she offered a consoling smile and continued, "You tell him I'll slit my own throat before I take anything less than half," her face then beamed, "and I want it in writing... son."

Po Tsai took the last sandwich and sat across from her, an amused expression on his face. "Our fleet is a couple hundred, I believe," he continued, "You know Zhèng Yī's brothers, Sì and San?" Their eyes met and she nodded even though she only knew of one brother. He continued, "If you count theirs, we are near seven hundred, total junks; about eight thousand men."

"Zhèng Yī and Zhèng Sì are brothers?" she feigned surprise. She knew exactly who they were. She made it her business to know all the clients that visited.

"Zhèng Yī is the oldest, number one son. Sì is the youngest, unlucky number four, and there is San and Jin in between." He nodded. She found herself nodding too. They looked at each other and discovered humor in their mirrored motions. Mógū looked away and suppressed a grin.

"The Black Fleet is as powerful and ferocious as our Red Fleet. Together they are no match for any navy out there. San and Jin's are yellow and blue. Not as forceful but still prevailing."

"So, which one would be mine?" The silence between them stretched out without an answer. She sipped the cold tea and changed the subject. "What about China? Now Qianlong is done do you think it will come down to a civil war?" Mógū had followed the politics in her area enough to know the last emperor was more preoccupied with artistic pursuits than running a nation. She also knew there were powerful men from four different families wanting to control and rule the developing areas before another emperor could be put in power. One of those families was the Zhèng family. Four sons! How the gods must love that family. She knew of their deadly reputation and their wealth.

"Changing a country's leadership is always difficult, especially now it's an entirely different family," Po Tsai continued after a moment's thought, "I would say yes; there will be blood. In my opinion there is no other alternative but to take control by force."

She nodded thoughtfully. "And the opium trade?"

Po Tsai chuckled. "A well-read woman, I like that. No wonder Zhèng Yī has his eyes set on marrying you. Don't you worry about politics, or your odious opium habit." He stood to leave. "You just worry about Zhèng Yī's proposal. It could be the offer of a lifetime, you know what they say about when opportunity knocks." She shrugged indifference and smiled.

Once he left, she made herself comfortable and began playing out the possibilities of becoming Zhèng Yī's wife. Why had she been so taken aback with his suggestion of a marriage? Was it reputation? Or did she picture herself a slave if she became a wife? The idea of a man telling her what to do and when was dismal. At least on the flower boat she had some free agency, or was that just an illusion of freedom? Was it the prospect of children? Pregnancy? What if she bore a daughter instead of a son? Would her husband be disappointed? What were the fears holding her back? Change she realized, it was doing something different than what she had always done, like the Manchu government's upheaval. The unknown is what frightened her.

The thought of settling down pressed down on Mógū's mind. The sad truth was, all her life decisions had been made for her. What if she were to make her own choices? Does an unwanted daughter from Guǎngzhōu deserve happiness? Love? What was love? Could love be found in one man, one partner?

Mógū fell into a deep sleep. She awoke in a dream where she was standing in a grove of populous lasiocarpa, their flowers in full bloom.

Sunlight struggled to get through the thick leaves causing small spears of light to cascade around her. It was cool and shady. Next to her stood Zhèng Yī, handsome and polished. She was holding a big bouquet of exotic flowers. She believed they were called tulips; bright red, their deep green leaves were sharp like knives. They looked menacing in her hand and it sent a little shiver down her back. When she looked up from the flowers, Zhèng Yī was no longer standing next to her, it was Cheung Po Tsai. His hair was braided down his back like a proper warrior. She was shocked awake at how handsome he had looked in an official looking Chinese Naval uniform, and the way he had been looking at her took her breath away.

She knew the dream was a good omen. Wealth and love would be hers if she married Zhèng Yī and became Cheung Po Tsai's legal mother.

Chapter Three – Wedding Day

Mógū peered out of the tent's small meshed window. There were more people than she had anticipated. Of course, every one of Zhèng Yī's family would be present, all the brothers plus uncles, aunts, cousins and all their heirs. She should have expected the large gathering.

The blossoms of the trees left a faint, fragrant smell. Spring had arrived. She was absently eating the dim sum and almonds that had been left for her. The lychee juice was cold and she hoped it left a red stain on her tongue to match the red paint on her lips.

This was her wedding day celebration. She smiled to herself knowing most virgins didn't get elaborate merriments such as this let alone an unwanted daughter from Guǎngzhōu who had, only recently, been working on a flower boat.

Fleeting images of her parents pinged in her head. Her beloved father who didn't care she was a girl. He had loved her anyway. As a humble fisherman, he had always provided for their family of three. She adored him and vice versa. A thrill ran down her spine when he waved from the little boat even though it was still quite a distance from the shore. The genuine smile he gave her as he glided into the shallow waters with his catch of the day filled her heart with affection and gave her a sense of security. Her mother's smile was never that pure.

As daddies often are to daughters, he was her hero. Her fondest memories were standing on the beach and catching sight of the dingy as it returned each night. The most heart-wrenching memory of her childhood was the night it didn't.

She was sure the boat would have been full of fish when they were heading back after a typical day at sea. At dusk a storm had roiled along the horizon and suddenly changed directions causing the boat to pitch and roll. It wouldn't have surprised anyone if all the men were more worried about losing the day's catch than their own safety. The boat capsized. The fish lost. The men drowned. Her father died.

When her mother had gotten news of the accident, she cried. The sobs seemed insincere somehow; a show for the family and friends. At the time, Mógū was nearly five years old. She watched her mother make a fuss as if she were on a stage.

Letting her mind drift back to the present, she peered from the muggy tent pretending her father was there, somewhere in the crowd. Once the agreement between them had been written up, and signed with witnesses, the arrangement for the wedding ceremony began. It took three months to gather all the necessary accoutrements for the most unnecessary event. She recalled Zhèng Yī's words when she brought up the fact neither of them really needed the official wedding ceremony.

"You deserve the most perfect wedding day of any queen," he had said, his eyes dancing.

"If half the money is mine, I should be able to say how it's spent."

He had laughed. "The agreement goes into effect AFTER the wedding, my dear," then added with a wink, "I'm still in charge."

She shook her head at the memory then glanced down at the deep red wedding dress. It was the loveliest dress she had ever seen, let alone owned. Layers and layers of red fabric adorned her body. A snug-fitting short red jacket with a rich gold embroidery was worn over the elaborate dress. She fingered the fabric and thought about how it could be taken apart and made into more sensible clothes, then laughed out loud. Why take it apart? She would wear it as an everyday dress. She would be the wife of Zhèng Yī after all and could wear what pleased her.

The eighteen-inch tall headdress was the most difficult part of the ensemble. She had practiced walking with it when it had arrived from mainland China. Gold cords with round beads hung down around her head. They swayed when she moved. Traditional brides kept their eyes adverted, but she was no typical bride. She had mastered walking with her head held high.

Her makeup had been painted on; lips as red as the gown. Gold flecks were smudged perfectly above her eyes. Her eyebrows had been drawn on with charcoal. The pure white face makeup had begun to dry and tightened her skin. Her black hair had been twisted upward and secured with long bamboo sticks giving the head piece something to attach it to. Once it was placed on her head, more bamboo sticks would be slid through little holes to secure it to her hair.

She hadn't thought of her mother for years yet here, today, the memory of her returned twice. Mother had taken another husband immediately after Father's funeral. It seemed baby brother had been born promptly after the wedding. Or maybe small children didn't have a correct sense of time. Either way, the baby was perfect in every way. Specifically, he was a boy. That was enough for her mother and new stepfather to spurn her. Yuzhòu (Universe) had completely replaced her when it came to her mother's attention. True to his name, he became the center of her parents' world.

Still lost in memory, she recalled an early morning when Mother had scooped her up and carried her out of the house. Mist hung low to the ground. The sun hadn't risen so it seemed the middle of the night. It was cold. With her chubby hands clasped around mother's neck she relished in the warmth of her body. Her head bobbed slightly on her mother's shoulder as they walked. For a minute, she dozed off and when she woke, mother was setting her on the hard ground. Her eyes adjusted and she looked around at her surroundings. They were at a temple of sorts. A long flight of stairs went up to a huge wooden door. She could see larger than life still figures of smiling men on either side.

"Crawl in there, daughter," Mother said, her voice sharp. She looked where mother had pointed. Her mother held open the small dull metal door with a shiny handle. She gave her daughter a nudge.

"I don't want to," the child whined as she arched her back and resisted. Her mother was strong and started to push her through the opening.

"Foolish girl, if you don't go in a wolf may eat you," her mom wrestled with her as she held the door open with her foot. "Go in!"

"Please, Mommy, no."

"You've got to stay here, crawl inside so you will stay warm," her mother's tone had gone flat. "You'll be fine, the nuns will come for you soon."

Suddenly a mewling came from inside the small opening. It pierced the early morning air and reverberated in the metal box.

"It sounds like a little sister is inside there." Her mother held the door open. She met her mother's flat stare, face twisted into a phony smile. Her eyes narrowed as she studied her mother and listened to the baby's high-pitched cry. *How could she know it was a sister? It sounded the same as Yuzhòu's wail.*

She hadn't realized that was the last blink of her innocence as she looked back at the path in which they had come. It was getting lighter and she could see the outline of the little fishing village as it came to life with the rising sun.

She glanced up at her mother for the last time and crawled in on her hands and knees. The baby was wrapped in a traditional serenity blanket. The door shut behind her; she heard her mother move the latch and the door tightened in its opening. She laid next to the baby and started shushing her, rubbing her hand over the baby's peach fuzzed head.

Sounds of steps coming nearer gave her a moment of anticipation. *Mother?* The door opened, sunlight streamed in and she got the first glimpse of the little babe cuddled next to her. A perfect set of red bowed lips and a face round as the moon. "You can be my little sister," she whispered to the babe, "I'll call you Chūntáo." She looked out into the face of a stranger.

"How many little mushrooms?" she heard a far-off voice ask.

"Two," the nun answered, still peering in, "a little one and a great big one."

A second head appeared in the small doorway. She was much older than the first but surprisingly the same. "Well look at that, a wee sprout and full-grown Xiǎo Mógū." The name had stuck, Mógū. Certainly, she had a name before the nuns dubbed her that, but she never could recall what it was, all the adults in her life had always just called her Girl or Daughter.

"Ready?" the younger nun asked as she reached in the receptacle and picked up the baby.

"Ready?" A voice brought Mógū back to the present, to the little tent and red dress. Her life began now. Time for her to take Zhèng Yī as a husband and secure her place as a pirate's wife.

The sun was setting, which is the most auspicious time of day to be married. Musicians began playing Dance of the Golden Snake, a traditional wedding song. Flower petals were being tossed down from children in trees, their giggles mixed with the music. Hundreds of candles had been lit and were placed around the gathering creating a magical atmosphere.

As Mógū stepped out of the bridal tent, she heard an audible intake of breath from the entire crowd. The reaction filled her with pride and settled her nerves at the same time. She walked slowly along the row

24

of silk that had been laid at her feet, then stepped onto the red and gold velvet divan that matched her dress. She sat as four men of equal height picked up the apparatus and placed it on their shoulders. They began to move through the throngs of people. Mógū kept her eyes forward and deliberately tried to look regal.

As she came to the front of the gathering, she saw Zhèng Yī, dressed in a traditional gold and red *dàguà* that closely matched her dress. She couldn't have imagined anything more impeccable than this had she dreamed the perfect wedding. Good fortune was indeed smiling down on her.

Chapter Four – Wedding Night

Mógū ate, drank, danced and socialized with influential people. She was introduced to Zhèng Yī's brothers, nephews and cousins as well as numerous people she felt confident she would never see again, business owners and men of means.

Eventually the guests began to leave. The staff started clearing away the leftovers from the feast.

"The real party begins now, my wife," Zhèng Yī said as he steered her to his bedchamber. Zhèng Yī's was the biggest room in the grand house. The furniture was elaborate hóngmù hardwood, ornately carved with protection dragons and auspicious symbols. There was a massive octagon-shaped rug, a large wardrobe and at one end, and farthest from the bed, the small table with several lit candles, their flames cast a soft, romantic light.

An opium pipe was beckoning to her from that corner of the room. She beelined for it, unbuttoning the wedding garment as she moved. With fluid motion she sat and prepared the thick substance all the while talking about the enchanted evening, knowing Zhèng Yī was only half listening. She lit the pipe from the candle on the table and inhaled.

The smoke ran through her riding the blood in her veins. She felt the relief from it, the relaxation from her shoulders to knees. She leaned down to take another toke when she gave a surprised yelp. There was a man on the bed. *Had he been there when she walked in?* He must have been or she would have heard the door.

She stared as the scene came together. Through the haze of the drug she realized it was Po Tsai and he was kissing Zhèng Yī. She shook her head trying to clear the image. Zhèng Yī and Po Tsai were definitely kissing on the bed. Zhèng Yī pulled Po Tsai's tunic off and started kissing down his chest.

"I love you," Zhèng Yī slurred.

"You're drunk," Po Tsai replied.

"You are too."

Mógū started to giggle, it bubbled in her chest and came out of her mouth in a full-blown laugh. The men, still holding each other, turned to look at her. Zhèng Yī's head rolled forward and he began to laugh too. That made Mógū laugh louder. Po Tsai looked between them and, with a pained look on his face, he climbed off the bed.

"I want some of that," he said as he moved towards Mógū, she held out the pipe to him.

"I want some of that," she answered casting her eyes to the bed where her husband removed his clothes. Po Tsai glanced at her and she saw the smirk in his eyes and half-cocked smile.

"Come here, wife," Zhèng Yī snickered as Po Tsai heated the pipe over the candle. Mógū was high and drunk. The bed seemed a long way and the red dress all of sudden seemed impossibly heavy. She shrugged off the top, but it was connected to the skirt part somehow, it all seemed to be holding her. She was trapped in an avalanche of red fabric. She looked around, panic taking hold as she tried without success to move towards Zhèng Yī.

It was Po Tsai's turn to laugh. "Woman, you're more fucked up than he is."

He deftly untied the back of the dress, his fingers fluttering around her waist and with great relief, the skirt and jacket dropped to the ground. *Free!* She giggled as she stepped out of the folds of fabric and gingerly made her way to the bed. Po Tsai accompanied her step by step. They swayed together moving awkwardly.

Zhèng Yī's smile was warm and loving, Mógū's heart swelled with affection. This was her new life; *he* was her new life.

"My family," he slurred as his arms settled around them both, "I luv yo."

All three laid back on the bed, Mógū tucked on one side of Zhèng Yī, Po Tsai on the other. She felt warm and safe, a part of something beyond just her. The opium had left her feeling euphoric; the whole day had seemed something from a dream. Surreal. Mógū's eyes closed with heavy lids. She knew Zhèng Yī was talking but the words seemed so far away. With some concentration, she was able to decipher what he was saying.

"...this union," Zhèng Yī continued, "we will be a force, unrelenting, unstoppable. This union is three now, it's a triangle, no, not a triangle, a pyramid, strong and robust. Together there is nothing we can't go after and have, from the shores of Trung Quôc to mainland China WE are the rulers, we command, we—"

"Go to sleep," Mógū heard Po Tsai chastise.

"Po Tsai, my boy, just listen to me for a moment, we have everything, everything we ever imagined. We did it!"

"Ya, ya, Zhèng Yī, stop," Po Tsai's words had a slight edge to them, "we're tired, I'm being serious, just stop talking and close your eyes."

Silence rippled through the room. Mógū's mouth twisted into a little grin as she fell asleep, her fingers laced together with Po Tsai's lying across Zhèng Yī's stomach.

Chapter Five – Wifely Duties

In Mógū's mind, the house she now lived in was nothing short of a palace. In some ways, it reminded her of the convent she and Chūntáo had grown up in. Multiple floors, large wooden doors kept closed, and echoes of footsteps if you didn't walk lightly.

The older, primary nun was always good to the girls. Mógū remembered her kindness in ways that, now she thought about it, indicated it had always been about profit for the convent. She wanted to believe they did it for the greater good but the girls all had a firm departure date. When they reached puberty, they were sold to one of the madams on the flower boats. It wasn't an argument nor was it open for debate, it was what it was. A fact.

Many of Mógū's childhood playmates had been sold to the same brothel and therefore created a deeper bond between the young ladies. Looking back, Mógū wondered if it was by design. Perhaps the nuns did have the girls' best interests at heart. Her mind wandered to the madam and the flower boat. She wondered how the young woman who had been accosted was doing, and which of the other girls survived, but mostly, her heart yearned for Chūntáo. She couldn't help but wonder what happened after the raid. She would have to ask around now she was a woman of means.

In her new grand house, a great hallway came to an intersection on the third floor where each of them had their individual bedchambers. Three floors! Zhèng Yī's room was the biggest and most spacious, with the largest bed and the opium table. Hers was adjacent and much smaller. Double doors allowed her to go out to a huge deck that Zhèng Yǐ's room also had access too. This area faced east, the most auspicious location for wealth and protection.

Po Tsai's room was across from Zhèng Yǐ's. It had large south facing windows, ideal for personal growth and romance. The fourth room was empty and when Mógū asked Zhèng Yǐ its purpose, he smiled and explained it was for the sons she would someday bear. It was the ideal location for family abundance and had already been decorated with opulent wooden furniture and bright blue and gold fabric.

The room was the same size as Zhèng Yǐ's, but looked bigger with only a few select pieces of smaller furniture. A hand carved cradle was the centerpiece. The idea of children gave Mógū anxiety. Yes, they had a staff of cooks and maids that would certainly bear the brunt of raising the offspring, but the idea of another being growing inside her left her full of apprehension.

She just would avoid pregnancy. For the years on the flower boat, the women would use a combination of liquid mercury and lead to avoid pregnancy. She had seen firsthand the damage that had done and avoided the concoction. Other options on the flower boats were the wild carrot called Queen Anne's lace that would end a pregnancy in its earliest stages. Fortunately, for her, it had never come to that.

Mógū's contraceptive of choice was olive and cedar oils mixed together. It was a trick many of the prostitutes used, lubing their client's hard shaft with it, promising more pleasure for them both but knowing the oils were a spermicide. She could also look into acquiring silphium, a fennel like plant that prevented pregnancy when ingested or used internally. It was expensive and hard to come by. It only grew in Cyrene and had to be imported but it would be a solid investment. She smiled to herself when she thought about the money she had married into; she could have anything she wanted now. The thought was more than comforting, it was euphoric.

The downside was the days were long. They stretched out and each morning filled Mógū with a bit of trepidation. She was bored. Her morning ritual involved wandering the hallways of the large house and then the grounds outside. After her morning walk, she would return to find the servants had left her breakfast. She would then dine alone.

"What do you expect me to do all day?" she complained to Zhèng Yī after their evening meal. She readied the opium pipe and took a long drag. Her head was foggy from the smoke and her belly full. She felt content in that moment, disconnecting from reality and able to speak freely.

"What do other women do all day?" he replied with indifference.

"How would I know, I lived on a flower boat?"

He lit the opium pipe and nodded his head in understanding but didn't offer a solution right away. "Once you have my son you will have plenty to do, Mógū. Be patient."

"Such a good idea," she said with an eye roll and a bit of sarcasm but then changed tactics.

Mógū retrieved the bottle of cedar oil from the night stand. She poured a small amount into her hands and moved them between his legs. "Yes, husband, a son," she mumbled as she rubbed the oil onto his penis. She loved that a man's penis had a mind of its own; men could be so easily manipulated through their manhood.

He removed his clothes and helped her out of hers. Their bodies came together with a little clumsiness, a side effect from the opium.

"What if I came to work with you?" she purred, "I could be very helpful, and I'm quick to learn new skills." She batted her eyes at him and rubbed his chest with both her hands while she raised her hips and matched the rhythm of his lovemaking.

"Mmm," he moaned.

"Is that a yes or a no?"

"Mmm, definitely a no," he leaned in and kissed her, wrapping his arms around her and pulling her close, "shh woman, kiss me." She did. They climaxed and collapsed exhausted.

"One reason why," she whispered as he was starting to doze off.

"One reason why what?"

"That I can't come with you while you raid."

"Oh, my beauty, my queen. I didn't marry you to put you in harm's way. It's not you, personally, don't be offended. Where I go, what we do, it's no place for a woman." He stroked her hair and continued, his tongue heavy and slightly slurred, "I never want you to look at me any other way than you do now. If you were to see the … the …" he appeared to be falling to sleep mid-sentence but then perked up and finished, "the brutality. What we do isn't pretty, it's quite messy and intense if I were being honest."

"I could handle it, I'm no ordinary woman," she said, cuddling deeper into his arms, rolling her leg over his and finding the perfect fit against his body.

"No ordinary woman, indeed," he mumbled as they fell asleep.

Before the sun rose, she heard Cheung Po Tsai and Zhèng Yī talking in the hallway. She got up to return to her bed and hopefully eavesdrop but she couldn't make out what was being said. She heard Po Tsai's door open and close again and Zhèng Yī's strong footsteps down the hall. It was easy to tell who was walking through the house. The strides of both men were as unique as they were and embodied how they lived. Zhèng Yī's steps were commanding, purposeful. He walked as she pictured him commanding his men, with decisiveness and power. Po Tsai on the other hand glided. He was virtually silent as he moved, light on his feet, lithe and agile. Wide awake now, she slipped into her room and dressed quickly.

Her plan was to follow Po Tsai undetected. She laid her ear against the door, waiting to hear his door open then close. Once he moved away, she counted to eight and opened her door as silently as she could. Staying near the wall in the darkest part of the hallway she moved with confidence through the big house in the pre-dawn blackness. She had a vague idea of where Po Tsai was heading and didn't want to be caught following him so she went down the service stairs instead of the grand staircase.

The sounds of the servants preparing breakfast, talking among themselves, floated up to her ears as she moved through their quarters. A door opened and shut and a young woman stepped out of a sleeping chamber; she yelped in surprise. Mógū held her finger to her lips and moved around the young woman to the servants' exit. Without regard for sound, she opened and shut the door moving into a courtyard full of chickens. They all began to squawk and waddle towards her expecting their breakfast. Mógū pressed herself against the wall, knowing Po Tsai should be just around the corner readying his horse for the day. The chickens increased their volume with full breakfast expectations. Po Tsai's horse gave a loud whinny and Mógū heard the hooves begin to move away.

Knowing Po Tsai would stick to the road, she darted from her hiding place and bound over the enclosure's fence to make her way through the trees where she knew the road would bend. Crouching low, she waited for Po Tsai.

Like clockwork the horse appeared. Indecision ran through her mind, *what now?* She stepped out onto the road with her hands on her hips, feet spread shoulder-width and her chin held high.

"Whoa," Po Tsai said bringing the magnificent beast to a stop. It pawed and side-stepped in irritation. Mógū could see it was clearly perturbed she was blocking the path. "Morning greetings, madam. You almost look like the lady of the house, but why would she be out here at such an hour?" Po Tsai asked merrily. Mógū remained quiet and motionless. "The. Lady. Of. The. House," Po Tsai said, a note of impatience in his tone. "Your job is a simple one, Mógū, stay in the house as your title implies."

"Take me with you," she said ignoring his comment.

Po Tsai chuckled. "What for?"

"I'm bored."

Po Tsai broke into a raucous laugh. "There's no entertainment for a lady where I'm going."

"You and I both know, I'm no lady."

Po Tsai's took in a long breath and let it out in a loud sigh. "There is no arguing that," he added, the notes of amusement back in his tone. The horse pawed the ground with impatience. "You may ride with me to the clearing, I'm not about to show up with a woman on my horse's tail. You may wave to us from afar. You may blow Zhèng Yī kisses, maybe he'll feel your presence." Po Tsai reached down and Mógū took his hand. He pulled her up to the back of the horse. It jumped forward, she almost lost her balance and impulsively wrapped her arms around Po Tsai.

"Where are you going?"

"To work." He laughed.

"I know that," she snapped back. "Work where? Which way are you sailing?"

The shake of his head and flip of the reins told her she would not be getting any more information from him. The horse took off in a run giving her the impression they had to make up for lost time. Mógū squeezed her thighs to the back of the horse as she dug one hand into Po Tsai's uniform and held the leather of the saddle with the other.

Chapter Six – Pirates' Life

When they reached the edge of the woods, Po Tsai pulled the horse to a slow canter and it circled to the left.

"Off," he commanded and she slipped from the back of the beast as it still moved in an arc. Once she had dismounted, he flicked the reins and they bolted away, neither looking back.

The dawn had begun to seep light across the waterfront. Mógū saw rows of men moving in unison performing the *tàijí quán* training. She knew the teaching included more than physical strength. It was also about mental preparedness as well as internal power. Quickly counting rows, she estimated there had to be a thousand men. Her eyes settled on Po Tsai as he rode up to Zhèng Yī. It was then she realized her husband was commanding all these kinsmen, they followed his every action, obeyed his every word.

All of the voices boomed, "*Uukhai!*" breaking the still of the morning. She watched as Po Tsai dismounted and handed his horse over to a lackey who led it to a small pen where Zhèng Yī's horse was already corralled.

Her heart swelled as she watched her husband pace in front of the rapt men, she knew he was speaking but couldn't hear what he was saying. After a moment, the battle cry rose again and the men dispersed with purpose and began to prepare the ships. Her gaze wandered along the harbor as she took in the activity. Each man seemed to know exactly what needed to be done. They reminded her of ants the way they moved on and off the vessels. When her eyes moved back to Zhèng Yī and Po Tsai they were engaged in a conversation.

Zhèng Yī's head turned towards her and she ducked behind a large rock hoping he hadn't seen her. A good wife shouldn't disobey her husband, she knew that, *everyone* knew that. It was the number one lesson the nuns repeated over and over; women obeyed. Her heart raced and she covered her mouth with her hand to slow her breathing.

She couldn't believe Po Tsai had told him she was there, the betrayal angered her, but the rage quickly turned to disappointment. She wanted Po to be her ally, but clearly, he was loyal to Zhèng Yī. What was she going to tell her husband? Had he seen her? Would he be angry she defied him?

After waiting a full minute, she slowly moved around the rock to peer at the harbor activity.

"Hello wife," Zhèng Yī said. He leaned against the rock, one leg kicked up in a casual stance, his handsome face, stoic. "Why are you here?"

"I want to go with you."

He shook his head. "It's not a good idea, I thought we went over this, you don't need to witness what I do, it's…" he stopped speaking, lost in thought.

"Husband, look at me." She stood in front of him and waited until his eyes met hers. "Half the fleet is mine. This was decided and—"

His mouth was set firm. "Mógū, please, I genuinely care about you. I don't want anything to happen to you."

"That's shit," she spat back. "You love Po Tsai more than you love me and you take *him* every time." Mógū felt the heat rise in her face, she bit her lip to stop speaking.

"Do not assume to know Cheung Po Tsai's role in my fleet nor in my heart," he barked. The flare in his temperament surprised her. This was the angriest she had ever seen him. "Know your place, woman!" She did not cower. They held each other's gaze for a heartbeat, then another.

"My place is by your side, husband."

Chapter Seven – Pillage

Mógū's efforts paid off, within an hour she was sitting on a hard, wooden stool in the small galley on the lead junk. Zhèng Yī's instructions were clear, don't move. Through the galley window she had a decent view of both port and stern.

She watched Zhèng Yī and Po Tsai work together as if in a coordinated dance. Zhèng Yī would call out something to Po Tsai and Po Tsai would make broad motions with his arms and the boat's mast would adjust or it would list slightly to catch the angle of the wind. Behind them, she saw the other boats had a spotter that gave the same physical commands to the men on the other junks. Because of that coordination, all six boats moved as one. Behind the group of these six were nine more groups of six, all moving in triangle formation. The sails appeared to spread out like a ribbon of scarlet blood bobbing in the waves.

Briefly she pictured all four of the Zhèng brother's fleets moving across the ocean together; red, black, blue and yellow, a prevailing force no navy would dare attack.

Nothing happened for several hours. They floated on the wind farther and farther from shore. Mógū was a little disappointed their voyage was boring. What were they looking for, what was it Zhèng Yī didn't want her to participate in? All of a sudden, Po Tsai's demi male voice carried to everyone's ears, "Brits!"

There was instant activity on the deck. Men sprouted up from below as the sails were adjusted for more speed. Behind them, the fleet started to spread from their singular line creating a wide presence on the horizon. She dashed to the other window; how did Po Tsai know the ship was British?

With all the men gathered on deck, her view became obstructed. She ventured out of the small room to get a better look promising herself she would duck back in the galley before Zhèng Yī noticed her.

They were gaining on the ship which was considerably larger than the junks. The sails had been cast high for maximum wind control. She could see by the way it sat in the water it was moving at a good clip. The energy from the men around her made her dizzy. Po Tsai continued to shout and made motions with his arms. Their six boats broke formation and spread out forming a V-shape. She could hear the splash and row, splash and row, of the oars plus the sails at full mast; there was no doubt they would catch up to the huge trade ship.

Hours later they still hadn't. Behind them, the fleet was completely spread out, the horizon billowing scarlet. Mógū found a spot where she could see the British flag whipping in the wind. The men had congregated together at the rails of the junk. Eventually, the sun started to go down, shadows grew long and the winds slowed. The rowing of the junks propelled their fleet to either side of the British trade ship.

A musket shot rang out above the din, then two, then it seemed like they didn't stop. The men on the trade boat were shooting at them. Ropes appeared from somewhere on deck. They were attached to large hooks. Two men cast these hooks to the larger trade ship. If they didn't stick, they were reeled in and cast again. Once they were secure, the crew pulled the two boats closer together until they were almost touching.

As soon as they were close enough, men seemed to pour off the junk onto the ship. Mógū could see the masts of the other three junks in their formation on the opposite side and knew just as many men were boarding the other side. Musket shots still rang out but were getting fewer and farther between.

Movement caught the corner of Mógū's eye. Zhèng Yī was swinging from a rope attached to one of the large masts. He dropped effortlessly onto the deck of the trade ship. The momentum of his drop propelled him forward, two steps and his sword appeared from the scabbard at his waist. On his third step, he wielded the sword with his right hand and with his left grabbed the hair of someone who was being held tight by one of their crew. With one stroke, he beheaded the man; Mógū concluded it was the captain.

Blood splattered on Zhèng Yī and the crewman who had been restraining the captain. Zhèng Yī still had his fingers in the man's hair and raised the severed head above his own, giving a loud cry of triumph. The men all answered with the same shout. Their voices seemed to carry along the waves. Mógū heard the other men as they shouted out the same roar.

The crew then set in motion taking down the men that remained alive. They were outnumbered and didn't stand a chance. Three or four men would handily carry one to the main deck where they were beheaded. A few pleaded and swore allegiance to the men, hoping to be spared the sword, and to Mógū's surprise, a few of the British men were bound and kept alive.

The number of Zhèng Yī's men on the boat now looked more like termites tearing into a piece of wood. Hundreds of men swarmed the deck taking control of the large ship. Mógū watched as Zhèng Yī slipped into the belly of their conquest.

With haste, she returned to the galley and found her stool. She sat as if she had been there the entire time even though her heart was racing and adrenaline made her woozy. The junk rocked and bumped into the other ship. She could see through the windows some of the activity. Just like this morning, each of the men seemed to know exactly what to do. No one had really paid any attention to her the entire day.

Finally, she began to breath normally again, the energy of the men and boat seemed to take on a business-as-usual air. The galley door flew open with a jolt. Zhèng Yī stood silhouetted by the now setting sun. A flash of relief pass over his face as he stepped into the room. Their eyes met. Mógū rose from her seat and strode across the small room in three steps. The air was thick with the tension between them. Mógū took a deep breath.

"Now you see why I didn't want you to come" Zhèng Yī began, "it's brutal, violent and—"

Mógū grabbed the front of his blood-stained shirt, and kissed him. She pressed her body into him. He tasted salty, a metallic tinge mixed in with the smell of blood and sweat. Without hesitation, he lifted her off the ground, her legs wrapping instinctively around his waist.

"Pardon," Po Tsai's voice interrupted their ecstasy, "Captain, everything is secure."

"Thank you, Quartermaster," Zhèng Yī said without taking his eyes off his wife. Mógū's eyes flitted to Po Tsai's. She gave him a sly smirk, *Quartermaster*. He grinned at her in return then winked before he closed the door and left them to their desires.

Chapter Eight – Blue Beads

Once they returned to He-Ong Kong with the British ship, Mógū realized the real work began. Unloading, inventorying and distributing the ships' contents was a week's worth of labor. Each participant in that day's raid received some compensation whether they boarded the British ship or not.

Zhèng Yī showed Mógū the ledgers that kept track of the payments to the men and their families. Some had been marked with special symbols indicating an extra portion for one reason or another, either a sacrifice they had made in the past or a debt that was still owed.

This particular ship hadn't made it to the Chinese port to do their bidding. The majority of the cargo was large wooden crates with an image of the British flag stamped on the ends. There were also several cannons and dozens of muskets. As for the ammunition, there were a lot of musket pellets but only six cannon balls. Mógū wondered why they hadn't used the bigger guns during the pursuit. Po Tsai explained there wasn't much flint or gunpowder and they were most likely going to use the weapons for trade once they reached Guǎngzhōu. None of it would necessarily be used for protection.

Po Tsai invited Mógū to the storage cave on Lantau Island where the merchandise was being cataloged. Its location was top secret. Only a few of the most trusted men accompanied them. Carts pulled by donkeys were loaded with the cargo from the ship to make the transferring easier. She tried to keep her expression neutral as they crested the threshold of the large cavern. Po Tsai had a lit torch that he held to several other wall torches. The light illuminated the large space.

Mógū inwardly gasped, there was so much loot it was overwhelming, "How do you know they were heading to Guǎngzhōu?" she asked Po Tsai still struggling to keep her face neutral.

"They were too far south to be going to Shanghai," he answered without much thought. She nodded, it made perfect sense. "Besides," he continued, "Guǎngzhōu is easier for the Brits to trade with. They are more hungry, eager to make a deal." An image of her birthplace and its people flashed in her mind as a momentary memory.

Two men came in pulling a flatbed cart with four large crates on top. They began to unload them near a stack of similar crates.

"Did you know I'm from Guǎngzhōu?" Mógū asked.

"That doesn't surprise me."

"What is that supposed to mean?" She gave a little uncomfortable laugh.

"It doesn't mean anything, just that you're tougher than the average Chinese girl, you know?"

"You associate toughness with Guǎngzhōu?" She could see her four-year old self standing on the beach waiting for her father's fishing boat to come in. Most of her memories from that age were helping with the day's catch, taking the fish from the holds, wrapping the heavy nets for storage and sloshing water in the hull, to clean the fish guts and then bailing the water back out.

There was an assumption the beach had been built up to an active trading harbor in the last twenty years; it probably didn't look anything like what she remembered. Indulging in the memory of her father, she was absentmindedly watching Po Tsai pry the slats off one of the wooden crates the men had just unloaded. He produced a small glass vial from it and held it up to the light from one of the wall torches.

"What's that?" she asked genuinely perplexed.

"Blue beads."

"What?" she motioned to see the glass container and he handed it to her. There were tiny blue pellets inside. "What do you do with them?"

"Make opium, of course." He laughed, moving away from her to help the men stack the crates with the others. She felt her body swoon, *make opium, of course* continued to repeat in her mind. He finished what he was doing and moved towards her. "It's the only way to ship it, like this, these little blue pills. Keeps it fresh for the clients. It's easy to heat and melt into the opium for pipes or you can leave it like this and add it to your tea. It's not the exact effect if you do it that way but—"

"Opium comes from the Brits?" her forehead was knotted in a confused expression.

"Sure, where'd you think it came from?"

"India."

"Yeah, of course it's grown there, south and east of the Bengal Bay but don't you know who controls India?"

"The British?" she guessed.

"There you go, tiger," he teased. She stared with a confused look on her face, he continued. "Here's how it all happened. A few decades back, the Brits were completely hooked on Chinese tea. Good stuff, right?" She nodded. "Zhu Zhilian, the emperor at the time, would only trade the tea for British silver, that's it, silver or nothing. There's something to an ultimatum, don't you think?" She nodded again as she quietly counted the number of crates with the British seal on them. So much opium right here under her nose. The thought gave her a rush from her groin to her brain; her palms felt moist.

Po Tsai continued to chatter on, "Eventually, the British ran out of silver to trade and had to come up with something because they were completely addicted to the Chinese tea. They were already controlling the port of Bangladesh so they began bringing opium to trade for the tea. It was a brilliant business maneuver, really. The wealthiest of our people got completely hooked on the substance and then began to buy it with the silver they had stock-piled from the tea sales the decade before." Mógū wanted to go smoke some opium right at that moment, her thoughts raced to Zhèng Yǐ's bedchamber where the little wooden table held the pipe and refined, ready-to-smoke opium. Her attention floated back to Po Tsai who was still talking. "... then they started trading anything for the opium, tea, guns, ammunition, whatever."

Mógū nodded, her own addiction raging in her gut. "Don't you worry someone may steal it?" she asked.

"Steal what?" Po Tsai replied looking confused. "The blue beads? No one wants to die over a bit of opium." He held out his hand.

She hesitated a moment before returning the vial to him. "Die?"

"Oh yes, I would run a thief through, right here, right now, wouldn't I?" Po Tsai asked the men who had just brought in another cart loaded with wooden crates. They both nodded without slowing down their pace.

After the ship had been completely unloaded, Mógū learned that it would be cleaned and repaired and then put up for sale. The income the ship would bring was more than Mógū had made working on the floating flower boat in a whole year. A percentage of the opium, weapons and ammunition were allocated to pay the rest of the men for their time and allegiance.

After their evening meal, Po Tsai slipped the little vial into Mógū's hand, "For your participation," he said.

"It's the first time a woman has been on the payroll," Zhèng Yī added with exuberance.

Mógū looked at the tiny blue pills nestled in the small glass bottle, then smiled and lifted her glass to the two men. "Here's to many more."

"Here, here," they both cheered and raised their mugs.

"More women or more raids?" Po Tsai asked and took a large swallow from his drink.

"Both," Mógū answered, her attention divided between the men who sat in front of her and her opium craving.

Chapter Nine – Close Call

Mógū kept the tiny blue pills hidden in her room. She added one to her morning tea and enjoyed the effects although she enjoyed smoking it after the evening meal with Zhèng Yī a lot more. A couple mornings in a row she noticed they had made her nauseous. She decided not to use them in the morning for a few days but the queasy stomach didn't seem to ebb.

Once she had missed her monthly cycle and the early morning sickness hadn't gone away, she began to panic. There was only the one time they had sex without the trusted cedar oil; it was on the junk after the take down of the British ship. The way she had wanted him, how aggressive she was with him was more than the turn on of the battle. Her body had been fertile.

Now her thoughts were filled with a way she could obtain local tansy root or daucus carota, the wild carrot, or even worm fern from Europe. Any one of these plants could bring menstruation back if the baby hadn't grown too big. The challenge now was to find it. Her first thought went to the cooks and other female staff in the huge house. In the months she had been living here, she hadn't cozied up to any of them. *No time like the present*, she headed to the kitchen to seek out the working women of the house.

Mógū learned the woman in charge name was Wu Jun. When she requested to speak with her, she was questioned why and what need of hers wasn't being addressed.

"I need a special, um… tea prepared," Mógū tried.

Měiyīng, another kitchen worker looked suspicious. "What kind of tea? Wu Jun doesn't need to be bothered over that. I'll make whatever tea you want."

"It needs a *special* ingredient," Mógū said with coyness.

"If you would please tell me what special ingredient you need, madam, I'm sure we can accommodate."

"It's medicinal. For women's cycles, delays in monthly—"

Měiyīng's eyes grew wide as understanding washed over her face. "Yes, ma'am. We may have some of that tea available," she hesitated and asked with trepidation, "For you?" Mógū's nod was almost undetectable. Měiyīng turned on her heel and exited the kitchen.

Mógū's eyes wandered the room. Měiyīng hadn't been kidding when she said they could accommodate special requests. Herbs and spices lined the walls. The shelves were cluttered with clay or porcelain containers with symbols painted to identify their contents.

The smell, the air, even the lighting seemed to take Mógū back in time. One of her favorite memories played in her mind. She and Chūntáo were working in the kitchen of the monastery. All the young women worked to keep the organization running smoothly. There was never a time in her life she didn't toil in some form from sun up to sun down, even on the flower boats, it was all business. In her mind's eye, she saw Chūntáo washing the dishes in the boiling water, making a game of getting them out quickly to minimize the burn on her fingers. She hopped from one foot to the other, the opposite hand raised above her head and sang out, "Two little tigers, two little tigers, running fast, very fast. One has no nose, one has twelve toes. Very weird, very weird." Mógū got caught up in the rhyme and danced with her broom picturing the twelve-toed striped cat.

A loud noise from the doorway startled them and they turned to see one of the nuns. She clapped her hands so loud it seemed to echo. The nuns often had a vow of silence and wouldn't speak under any circumstance so they would make elaborate hand gestures and use their body language to get their point across. The nun standing in doorway drew her mouth down into an ugly grimace and shook one long crooked finger at them. Chūntáo jumped towards her and curled her hands out like a cat's claws then gave a loud cat sounding screech. The nun reached out her own hand, fingers bent claw-like and gave a realistic sounding feline hiss, her expression matching the sound then stormed off.

The two girls looked at each other and burst out laughing. It was one of the only carefree moments in Mógū's childhood she could remember.

The sound of Wu Jun clearing her throat got Mógū's attention and brought her back to the kitchen. Wu Jun and Měiyīng stood side by side, their expressions stoic.

"Měiyīng tells me you need a root to help your cycles be more regular," Wu Jun stated with authority.

"That's right."

Wu Jun nodded. "I've made arrangement for Cheung Po Tsai to take us to the market and get the necessary roots for the black tea."

Mógū shook her head. "Not Po Tsai, he doesn't need to accompany us."

"He does," the two women replied in unison.

"He doesn't."

"You are a married woman. He does." Wu Jun was adamant. On cue, Po Tsai entered the kitchen.

"Let's go ladies, I don't have all day," he said with notes of irritation.

"You don't have to go," Mógū retorted.

"Oh, but I do," Po Tsai sighed, "the law is clear, you must be accompanied by a man while you are in the city."

"Isn't there another man who could go?"

"Oh sure, honey, I'll go get Zhèng Yī. I'm sure he would love to take you to the market to get a root that will terminate the life of his unborn son," Po Tsai remarked with sarcasm.

The comment felt like a punch to the gut, she couldn't believe Měiyīng and Wu Jun had told him her business. Mógū glared at each of them. After a moment, she said, "That's it, let's go."

It was a tight fit, but the four of them were able to cram into the horse-drawn rickshaw.

"For the record, I'm helping you only because I prefer to be Zhèng Yī's only heir," Po Tsai said softly into Mógū's ear.

She turned and looked at him. "Of course, Po Tsai, you are, naturally, the child of the household."

He grunted a reply. They rode in silence the remainder of the way.

54

Once they arrived in the massive market, the horseman helped the ladies from the carriage.

"We'll be back," Mógū called over her shoulder and thought how stupid it was Po Tsai had to come with them just for him to nap while they shopped the market. She followed Wu Jun and Měiyīng into the throngs of people. The two women seemed to know exactly where they were going.

They found the shop they needed and Wu Jun began to inspect some of the hard, black roots on display in a woven basket. Mógū stood a few feet back and looked around at the other wares for sale.

A woman near her sucked in her breath audibly and then exclaimed, "Pinyin!" Mógū looked around to see what the surprise was only to meet the stare of her old friend, Chūntáo. "Big sister? Is it really you?" Wu Jun and Měiyīng as well as everyone else in earshot had stopped what they were doing and stared at the two women. Time seemed to stand still as Mógū processed the woman in front of her. Surely, she wasn't seeing an apparition, this shopkeeper was real, but how could it be Chūntáo?

"I thought you were dead."

"Likewise," Chūntáo replied.

Tears stung the back of Mógū's eyes. "How? Where? What?" she stammered, "I saw you get, the sword, the blood..."

"Wicked, right?" Chūntáo exclaimed pulling down her blouse. "Look, clean through." She showed Mógū a puckered scar right in between her breasts. "All the gods were smiling down on me that day," she said with excitement, "and today too as my big sister and best friend has returned to me." She looked at the matronly, plump Wu Jun and back to Mógū, "You ladies working?" she asked, with a confused tone.

"Yes," Měiyīng answered at the same time Mógū shook her head, no.

"I'm not in that line of work anymore, you?" Mógū heard Měiyīng gasp as the young woman realized what Chūntáo had been implying.

"No, I'm much too old and fat for that now," Chūntáo said with a pointed look in Wu Jun's direction.

"They aren't prostitutes either, they are my cook and cleaning maid," Mógū answered. Wu Jun and Měiyīng took turns shaking and nodding their heads.

"You have a cook and cleaning maid?" Chūntáo let out a huge, bright laugh.

"I married into the Zhèng family," Mógū explained.

"*The* Zhèng family? You didn't?!"

"I did," Mógū smiled, "crazy, right?"

"Aren't they a bunch of murdering thieves?"

"Well, I guess, that's one way of putting it. I don't know how to answer that, but Zhèng Yī is quite nice. He's good to me. So is Po Tsai. We live—"

"Who?" Chūntáo interrupted.

"Zhèng Yī's heir."

"He has a son?"

"Not exactly, it's… well… it's complicated. He's an ally, for the most part."

"Dear sister, we certainly have a lot to catch up on, don't we?" Chūntáo shook her head with a smile playing at the edge of her mouth. She reached out to take Mógū's hand.

"I've missed you," Mógū said welcoming the physical contact with her long-lost friend, "I'm so grateful you're alive."

"You and me both," Chūntáo grinned.

"I hesitate to leave, little sister. It's been too long. Perhaps you should come back and stay the night with us," Mógū suggested. Wu Jun and Měiyīng looked horrified.

"That sounds like a fabulous idea," Chūntáo exclaimed, "yes, let me close up shop and I'll go."

"Oh, let's not forget, we still need the root," Mógū said, "What do we owe you?"

"It's my treat," Chūntáo replied, "for old time's sake." She wrapped a generous amount of the root in burlap and tied it with a string. "Which one of you ladies is it for?"

"I'll take it, thank you," Mógū said as she slipped the bundle into a deep pocket.

Mógū's heart was full as they all walked back to the carriage with Chūntáo. She never believed she would have seen her little sister again; the love she had for her had left a hole in her heart she hadn't realized was a constant pain, but now it seemed the world was set right.

Chapter Ten – Sisters' Reunion

"No, no, absolutely not." Po Tsai's jaw was set firm.

"You don't make the decisions for me, in fact, I don't want you dictating any options for my life. Let's not forget, I'm the lady of the household, 'Mommy', remember?" Mógū was hoping her tone left no room for argument with Po Tsai, but of course, he bucked at the idea of Chūntáo returning with them. The village streets were crowded, bustling with people selling or shopping. Mógū didn't necessarily want to make a scene.

"There's not enough room." Po Tsai indicated towards the carriage.

"You can sit up front with the driver," Mógū shrugged her shoulders as if it were an obvious solution.

"Or on my lap," Chūntáo added, eyeing Po Tsai with a wicked grin plastered on her full lips, which caused a grin to cross Mógū's mouth too.

Po Tsai shouted, "I told Zhèng Yī it wouldn't be worth it for—"

"Just stop," Mógū snapped.

"Women!" Po Tsai threw up his hands in defeat.

She followed Po Tsai moving him away from the women. The driver opened the carriage door and assisted the ladies in. "Let's get something clear between us, Po Tsai," Their eyes met and anger flared in Mógū's soul. "I make my decisions. I don't need a man to tell me what to do or how to do it, do you understand me?"

"Let's get something clear," he snapped and spat on the ground between them, "you're a woman, female, the lesser sex, you're incapable of making proper choices without a man's direction—"

"Shut up!" Mógū exploded, "I've had it with you, you arrogant, spoiled child. Really, who do you think you are?" Her voice escalated and she was sure people were watching but she didn't care. "You come into my life, almost kill the most precious person in the world to me. Steal me away from everything I've ever known—"

"Rescued you," he interrupted.

She held up her hand to silence him and continued. "You took me from everything I've ever known only to order me around like a servant. You *are* Cheung Po Tsai the kid, Po the *child*. You're immature, unreasonable and...and..." she stumbled on her words, the anger getting the best of her. She took a deep breath and continued. "Let me reiterate, I'm not your mistress, nor you wife, I don't work for you, you work for me, got it?" They stared at each other for a long, tense moment. "Just remember, I didn't ask for this, this wasn't *my* decision."

"Well, that's something we have in common," he snapped at her, "it wasn't my decision either. I was following orders, looking out for the greater good of Zhèng Yī."

"Oh, don't you dare go noble on me." She was shaking with indignation. "You were looking out for the greater good for yourself. You know it. I know it. Now get up there with the driver, sit down and shut up."

"I hate you," he mumbled as he climbed onto the driver's bench of the carriage.

"Likewise," she retorted and turned on her heel to join the other women. She paused at the door of the carriage and glared into the street at the men and women staring at her, the men with their looks of disgust and the women, stealing glimpses from under their oversized bamboo hats. "Show's over," she snapped and climbed in, slamming the door harder than necessary. Once seated it took Mógū several moments to calm down, she breathed deep and deliberate, her hands still shaking while the carriage began to move. "My apologies," she said to the three women.

"Hush now, sister, you're no proper lady. We don't expect an apology," Chūntáo replied taking Mógū's hand. "He deserved that, clearly. Even Měiyīng and Wu Jun know he's the one out of line."

"I don't know that," Měiyīng spoke up and the other three turned to look at her. "I mean, in some ways, he's right, we *are* women. Men should be telling us what to do and how to do it, otherwise, how will we know what they want?"

Mógū felt her stomach clench, bile churned and she took a deep breath. "We may be women, but we're not inferior. Just because we're born female doesn't mean we have to wait on them hand and foot."

"Sure, we do, if we don't, who will?" Měiyīng's innocence would have been funny to Mógū if she hadn't been so outraged.

"This is the problem with society, we aren't valued for all we have to offer," Mógū's words were clipped and sharp. "Anything a man can do, I can do."

"She can even pee standing up," Chūntáo chimed in.

"Pff!" Měiyīng snorted and turned her attention to the passing landscape. "Vulgar beast," she mumbled under her breath. Mógū turned and looked at Chūntáo who shrugged without additional comment.

"It won't ever change," Wu Jun stated flatly, her attention diverted to outside the carriage window, "not in our lifetime. It is our lot in life to serve men, it's how it's always been, it's how it will always be."

"That attitude just infuriates me," Mógū answered.

"You can't do the things men do," Měiyīng added not looking at any of them, "women are not as strong or as smart."

"Oh, I disagree," Mógū said, "You say that because you were told that, but we *are* strong, we *are* smart, much more than we are given credit for." Her eyes met Chūntáo's.

"I agree with big sister," she affirmed, giving Mógū's hand a little squeeze, "besides, there's power with the treasure between our legs, ladies."

"Pah!" Wu Jun rolled her eyes; with a snap she produced a hand fan and began waving it in front of her face. Měiyīng turned a deep red and diverted her attention to her feet.

Mógū gave a little laugh and patted her friend's knee. "You have such a way with words my wise friend."

Chapter Eleven – Homecoming

Once they arrived home, Mógū opened the door of the carriage before the driver could get down and do it for them. She watched while Měiyīng climbed out. Po Tsai nimbly jumped down. The driver appeared and assisted Wu Jun.

"I've got it," she clucked, waving away his offered hand. He took her by the elbow as she descended. "Bring the fares to the kitchen," she ordered him as she started up the steps. He hustled and busied himself with the packages from the back of the rickshaw.

Before Mógū was completely out of the carriage, the front door of the house swung open and Zhèng Yī stepped out.

"Where have you been?" he asked, his jaw taut, forehead knit. Mógū climbed out from the carriage. Měiyīng and Wu Jun moved around him and disappeared into the house. Zhèng Yī's attention turned to Mógū while Chūntáo descended the small portable stairs. "Who is she? What have you been doing all day?"

Mógū couldn't tell if his face had turned angrier or just more confused.

"This is my little sister, Chūntáo," Mógū said to her husband while giving a little respectful bow. Chūntáo followed suit and bowed to the master of the house as well. Po Tsai headed to the door taking the steps two at a time.

"Stop!" Zhèng Yī said, holding his arm out to restrict Po Tsai from entering the house. "Little sister?" he said eyeing Chūntáo, "she's twice as big as you are, and half your age, clearly she is not."

"You don't define my family," Mógū replied as she raised her eyes to meet his. She glared at him and his harsh remarks. "We *are* sisters, we were raised by the same—" she hesitated and stumbled on her words, "convent."

"Questions. Why is she here, one, and two, somebody tell me where have all of you been?" he glared at Po Tsai, then his wife.

"To get Chūntáo," Mógū spoke up at the same time, Po Tsai rolled his eyes.

"Lies," he spat, "she went to the market to buy the root, this piglet just happened to attach herself to your wife." Chūntáo made a face and an oinking noise towards the men.

"Root?" He shook his head in frustration. "What kind of root do you have to travel to the marketplace for?"

Po Tsai opened his mouth to speak, Mógū shot him a look of daggers, as Chūntáo answered, "It's concerning a feminine nature," she said primly and smiled at the men, "private women's stuff."

Mógū was still glaring at Po Tsai but felt a chuckle in her chest, she had truly missed her friend.

"Did I ask you?" Zhèng Yī snapped, his face was pinched and turning an ugly shade of red.

"You didn't *not* ask me," she answered still smiling the forced, fake grin.

"Chūntáo will be moving in with us as my personal assistant," Mógū said, her mouth turning into a smirk to complement Chūntáo's.

"I will?" Chūntáo's whole face beamed with excitement. Po Tsai threw his hands in the air and made a noise of frustration. He pushed past Zhèng Yī and into the house.

Zhèng Yī's mouth hung slightly open and he blinked twice, slowly. Mógū could see he was processing how to rebuke her. Before he could, she pushed on with her declaration. "Yes, she will. This house is half mine and—"

"It is?" Chūntáo's voice was high pitched and giddy. "Really? Half yours?"

"Psst," Mógū hissed towards Chūntáo. Not-so-fond memories of little sister's wisecracks during work or worship pinged into her mind as she sighed and returned her attention to Zhèng Yī. "At this time, I feel I require an assistant for my daily duties and responsibilities."

"What responsibilities? You aren't required to do anything."

"Hence lies part of the problem in which Chūntáo will be assisting me." Their eyes were locked. Mógū learned long ago the alpha dogs held their stares longer than the betas. She saw Zhèng Yī's mouth open and close as if he were still formulating his reply. She knew she would have her way. He moved his eyes to Chūntáo and Mógū felt a small victory in his surrender before he spoke.

"We'll talk after supper," he turned and took the four steps of the porch in two long strides. The door swung closed with force but was too big to properly slam.

"He must be late for his suck off appointment," Mógū mumbled with irritation and a touch of jealousy.

"Suck off, like?" Chūntáo made a motion of fellatio with her open mouth and rolling her eyes upward.

"Yeah," Mógū answered with a snicker, "let's go through the back." She guided her friend around through the chicken coop and into the servants' quarters. She continued as they walked. "They needed me, that's why they kidnapped me."

"Who needed you?"

"Think little dummy," she slapped Chūntáo on the back in an affectionate way and then put her arm around her sister's shoulders. "I missed you even though you are dimwitted. Zhèng Yī needed a wife to adopt Po Tsai to make him a legal heir."

"Couldn't he have just asked?" Chūntáo said, looking even more confused.

"He did," Mógū replied, "I said no. I didn't realize he was—"

Chūntáo squirmed out of Mógū's grasp and punched her in the arm. "Who's the dimwit now? Eeeyyy, how are you so smart and so stupid at the same time?"

"Just one of my many talents," Mógū answered with a laugh.

They had walked through the servants' quarters and stood in a large pantry. Mógū took a half empty bottle of rum from a high shelf and they turned to walk out as Wu Jun walked in. She held out her hand. "I've got water on for the tea."

Mógū dug into her pocket and produced the root. "Would you like Jasmine" or Oolong?" she asked Chūntáo.

"I'll be drinking the rum." She motioned to the bottle in Mógū's hand.

"Oolong will be fine, thank you," Mógū said with a slight roll of her eyes. Wu Jun bowed and left.

"Come on," Mógū said and led the way to the third floor. Walking down the long corridor she motioned to a long green ribbon hanging on Zhèng Yī's door, it was the signal Zhèng Yī didn't want to be disturbed. "They are having a suck fest, that's too bad, I was hoping for some opium today," she winked at Chūntáo.

"You don't make any sense. You can't have any opium because your husband is having sex with his adopted son?" Their eyes met and they began to giggle. Mógū covered her mouth and motioned for Chūntáo to be quiet and follow her in the empty room across from Zhèng Yī's.

"From here, we can see when Po Tsai leaves," Mógū said in hushed tones once they were in the spare room. She looked around. "I guess you'll sleep in here. I mean Zhèng Yī adopted Po Tsai, I'll adopt you."

"I don't have to sleep with you, do I?" Chūntáo countered with an exaggerated eye roll.

"Oh, you would just to have a room as fine as this one, don't kid me," Mógū joked as she poured the rum and handed it to Chūntáo.

"Bet your sweet coochie." Chūntáo beamed as she took the rum and drank it in one gulp. "More, please," she said, face contorted from the hard liquor. Mógū laughed and poured more. There was a light rap on the door. The two women froze, cups raised halfway to their lips.

The door opened slowly and Wu Jun poked her head in. Once she saw the women, she eased into the room with a tea cart full of dim sum, two boiling kettles of water and several tea infusers.

"This one is for you." She motioned to the largest infuser in the basket. "There is more here." She then pointed to a small ceramic jar with a lid on it. "I think this is the right amount, but every woman is different." Mógū nodded. "Let me know if there is anything else I can do to assist you. There are herbs for the pain, expect a lot of blood and—"

"Yeah, yeah," Chūntáo interrupted, "we get it. We got it, thank you."

She moved to the door and opened it, indicating for Wu Jun to leave. Just then Zhèng Yī's door opened and Po Tsai stepped out. Mógū caught his eye then glanced at Zhèng Yī who was closing the door. She could tell by the way he moved he was high. The acrid stench of opium slipped through the doorways causing Mógū's heart to race just a bit, envy flooded her face as she turned back to Po Tsai who stared at the tea cart. Their eyes met; his mouth turned into a wicked opium induced smirk. He staggered across the hall into his own room. Mógū closed the door and drank the rest of her rum. Chūntáo had already helped herself to the dim sum.

"This is good," she said, stuffing a dumpling into her mouth. Mógū poured herself more rum then took a piece of chicken from one of the plates and popped it in her mouth. "So why did you want the tea again?" Chūntáo asked.

Mógū shook her head. "To terminate a pregnancy." She picked up another chicken dim sum and ate it.

"Yes, yes, I'm not a dumb ninny goat, but *whose* pregnancy?"

"Mine, of course," Mógū poured the water and added the large bamboo infuser. A dank, rotted smell floated up from the cup. Mógū fought the urge to gag.

"Why would you do that?" Chūntáo asked, holding her hand over her nose.

"I don't want a baby," Mógū replied flatly.

"They are only babies for a year."

"They are a long-term commitment I don't want. I like smoking opium, sleeping until midday," Mógū rambled, "having another human being inside of me is disturbing somehow and besides, I enjoy going out on the junks with Zhèng Yī, it's … exciting."

"I'm here now, I'll help you. I'm your personal assistant, remember?"

Mógū rolled her eyes and shook her head then picked up the cup of foul-smelling tea. "Wait, sister, listen to me," Chūntáo grabbed Mógū's wrist and brought her face so close Mógū could smell the rum on her friend's breath. "I get the feeling you and Po the kid aren't exactly chummy." Mógū shook her head, her face crinkling into an exaggerated frown. "So have the baby, take the upper hand. You will have Zhèng Yī wrapped around your little finger if you produce a son for him."

"What if it's a girl?" she subconsciously placed her free hand over her stomach.

"Then we raise her up, put her in the kitchen with Wu Jun and get rid of that Měiyīng girl, she's a bit bothersome anyway."

Mógū began to giggle, then laugh. "Chūntáo, you are a gift, you know that?" She returned the cup to the tea service and took in a deep breath. The decision felt like a relief somehow and she continued to snicker.

"Gift? That may be an exaggeration," Chūntáo said then took a long draw from the rum bottle and handed it to Mógū, her face puckered from the strong liquor, "maybe more of a jinx."

"Good luck charm?" Mógū took her own swallow from the bottle. "That's it, little sister, you're my lucky yin."

Chapter Twelve – Another Close Call

Mógū made sure Chūntáo was comfortable in her new room. There had been plenty of beautiful items to choose from in the secret cave where the treasures were kept. Po Tsai had refused Mógū's request that Chūntáo accompany them. Mógū was put out, but not wanting to make a scene, she announced she would just choose the most luxurious items for her new assistant, and she did.

Chūntáo took over Mógū's household duties, running it with more efficiency and unyielding routine than Mógū had ever been interested in applying. When Mógū returned with the men after their raids, she found elaborate food prepared, hot water for a bath ready and her night clothes clean and laid out.

"How did I ever survive without an assistant," she said one night as she relaxed in the steamy water, eyes closed.

"Poorly," Chūntáo answered as she busied herself with the nightly duties.

"I think Po Tsai is trying to kill me," she confided one night as Chūntáo worked on braiding Mógū's long hair. This had become a regular ritual, once Mógū was done with her bath. Chūntáo combed out Mógū's hair and then put it in tight plaits for the next day.

"Kill you how?"

"Zhèng Yī says I'm a distraction on his boat—"

"A distraction?"

"Yes, he says he gets too worried about me and pays more attention to what I'm doing than to what he should be doing."

"Ah, that's sweet, but what does that have to do with Po Tsai trying to off you?"

"I'm getting to that," Mógū said, "Zhèng Yī put me and Po Tsai on a different boat and he's supposed to keep watch over me or something like that."

"And?" Chūntáo questioned with a bit of sarcasm.

"Po Tsai told me the best captains stand on the front of the junks while they're moving."

"Mm-hmm." Chūntáo sighed and continued her task.

"It makes sense as the view is unobscured and I can see what the other boats in the fleet are doing but it's slippery and there's nowhere to hang on. If the junk hits a big wave the wrong way, it's jarring. I've almost fallen a couple times."

"Don't be such a ninny, just don't stand there. Stand somewhere safe."

"Well that's the thing, there isn't a place for me to just stand. All the men have their jobs and I don't want to be in their way and I certainly don't want to be with Po Tsai the whole day."

"Could you fasten some sort of hold just to make it safer?" Chūntáo asked as she finished Mógū's hair.

"It's a good idea but I would have to make it portable or affix the entire fleet since we don't have the same boat every time, which isn't a horrible idea if indeed all the best captains stand there, but I'm not even sure that is the truth." Chūntáo offered her a half-full mug of rum which she took gratefully. "I think he has me there hoping I will fall off and drown, then he will be Zhèng Yī's sole heir and things can go back to the way they were before." She drank the contents of her cup in two swallows.

"Did you tell him you didn't drink the tea?"

Mógū shook her head, and blinked hard, the liquor had caused her eyes to water. "Not a chance," she choked out, "he can be as surprised as Zhèng Yī when I make the announcement."

"When are you going to do that? I really want to be there to see Po Tsai's face," Chūntáo guffawed. Finished with the hair task, she retrieved Mógū's boots from beside the tub. She then picked up the boot polish and rag and worked on cleaning them.

"Wu Jun says to wait three moons before I say anything," Mógū explained as she poured herself another rum. "Apparently if a woman is going to lose her baby that's the most common time."

"I wonder sometimes if you are even pregnant, you don't act like it," Chūntáo commented.

"How am I supposed to act? Fat? Miserable?" Chūntáo shrugged and continued to clean one of the boots. "That's it!" Mógū exclaimed.

"What's it?" Chūntáo said with a bit of frustration.

"The boots," Mógū took the boot Chūntáo wasn't working on and turned it over, studying the heel. She took a knife from the service tray and carefully pried the heel off. "What if I put nails through the heel so they created a sharp, jagged bottom. I could stomp my feet into the wood and it would, in theory, hold."

"In theory." Chūntáo laughed and motioned for Mógū to hand over the second boot.

She did but continued to ponder the footwear. "I think it would be easy enough. Tomorrow I'll go to the blacksmith and see if there are small enough nails to go through without splitting this wood part."

"There you go," Chūntáo said without looking up, "problem solved."

The following day the crew wasn't planning on sailing but to inventory, distribute and store the items from the ship they had subjugated the previous afternoon. Mógū wouldn't be needed until all the items were removed from the ship, then she would be expected to take a large ledger, ink and quill to make notes for the men's allocation of the booty.

For the most part, she had collected all her wages in the blue pills. She definitely preferred them after they were processed into the tar-like substance for smoking. Chūntáo had no problem indulging with her on a regular basis. Mógū had acquired her own pipe and often they would stay locked in Chūntáo's room until dawn, smoking opium and drinking rum.

Early the next morning, she slipped down to the stables where the blacksmith had his bellows and irons. She watched patiently as he pounded a horseshoe flat, heating it, pounding it, then heating again to repeat the process. It was toasty warm in his work quarters and the repetitive noise of the metal hammer was mesmerizing. When the blacksmith finished with one of the horse's shoes, he turned to Mógū.

"Is there a reason you're watching me work?"

"Um, er, yes," Mógū was flustered for a moment. "I need help with my boots."

"I'm not a cobbler," his voice was firm and matter of fact.

"Yes, of course you're not, and I know this, but I would like some metal nails put through my heels here." She bounced on one leg and took off a boot, then popped the heel off and presented it to the man.

"Why would you want to do that?"

"Well, when we are out on the ship, it would be nice to be able to dig into the wood a bit so I won't slip. If the nails were small enough you could—" the man was nodding and held his hand out to her.

"I get it, leave them with me."

"Leave them? I don't have any other shoes."

"I can't fix them if I don't have them, and my priority right now is finishing these horse shoes. I should be able to get to them late today or tomorrow, perhaps even—"

"No later than tomorrow," Mógū interrupted, she pried the second boot off and handed it to him, "I'll compensate you, don't worry about payment but I do need them as soon as possible."

"Yes, ma'am." He took the boots and set them on a large work table and resumed his task with the horse shoes. She tip-toed out of the shack and back to the house in her bare feet.

Without thought, Mógū met Po Tsai and the inventory crew to do their task of sorting and storing the items from the ship. She wore the only other footwear she had, a pair of house slippers.

Po Tsai noticed immediately. "Where are your boots?"

"I was running late this morning, so I just kept on my *tuōxié*."

Po Tsai shook his head and mumbled under his breath, "Women."

The most recent ship was mostly full of weapons. Swords, scabbards, cannons and pistols as well as crates and crates of ammunition. Mógū dutifully wrote each item in the ledger and grouped it so it could be stored.

An angled, shorter sword nestled in a leather scabbard caught her attention. It appeared to be forged from one piece of metal, the handle was wrapped in soft, supple leather with a small white tassel which hung from the end of the wrap. Instead of noting it in the weapons section of the ledger, Mógū flipped over to the payroll tab and marked it as her payment for that haul.

She looked at the other men's payroll markings, and turned the page back noting the marks that represented gold, silver, pistols, salt, silk, rum, tea and blue beads. She turned several pages forward and scanned the rows of entries. Zhèng Yǐ's name registered in her head and she used her finger to trace down the column noting the payments he had received dating backwards from the current date. To the side of Zhèng Yǐ's was Po Tsai's record. It occurred to her neither had been paid in blue pill opium even though she knew they were indulging in it as much, or more, as she and Chūntáo.

With a new determination, she scanned the pages again. No one was being paid with the blue pills except for her. Upon further inspection, she realized the opium wasn't even being inventoried in the ledger, there was no trace of it except on her column for payroll payment.

Glancing around, she noticed everyone was doing their jobs without the need for supervision. This gave her the opportunity to accrue a few items for herself. She hefted one of the long-barreled guns up to her shoulder looking down the sights, then put it back with the others. The handheld pistol was much heavier than she expected but she liked the feel of it better than the cumbersome rifle. She picked up a different one that had a leather holster. It slid effortlessly from its case, the wooden butt of the gun fitting in her hand perfectly.

She went back to the current page and added the symbol for a pistol in her column, then a case of ammunition as well. Without haste, she untied the sash around her tunic and threaded it through the pistol holster and the cutlass scabbard. With a little adjustment, they both sat perfectly on her hips. Unexpectedly, the weapons felt natural. She moved with a confidence she hadn't had when she woke that morning. As she worked among the men, she took notice they were all armed heavily, each with their own weapons of choice strapped to their persons.

Around midday, Po Tsai approached Mógū and asked to the see the ledger. Surprised but not taken aback, she handed it over aware he had seen the pistol and cutlass at her waist. He immediately turned to the paid-out section of the book.

"You don't want your precious opium this go?" he asked with a sneer.

"Of course, I'll take that too. In addition to what's recorded." His eyes narrowed at her. "I don't see that in anyone's records but I know there is plenty to go around."

"Listen lowly woman, you need to remember your place—"

"I am Madam Zhèng Yī," she interrupted, "your maternal figure in every sense of the word. Let's definitely not forget who I am, in fact, let's define it." The power that overcame her as she stood up to Po Tsai was incredibly stimulating. Some of the other men had paused to watch the standoff. "I will take what I earn and what I need, you don't dictate to me my job or my compensation. If anything, I will communicate to you what items will go where and you will pay attention and follow orders."

"I take orders from Zhèng Yī," he snapped.

"You will conform and answer to *me*," her indignation was rising in her gut and she was fully ready to argue.

"Listen here, *woman*, I doubt you have the mettle to use those weapons. It would be better if you just inventoried them and put them away before you hurt anyone." Mógū pulled the cutlass from the scabbard at her waist and held it towards Po Tsai. "Stop! Put it down," he scolded, "You are a wife, female, a little girl. You will never be a pirate like us," Po Tsai snapped, he clearly had not taken notice of their audience, "you are nothing."

Mógū scanned the faces of the men who had gathered around them. "Nothing?" She was outraged but maintained her composure for the men who watched. "I will be a greater pirate than any of you," her tone was solid and serious maybe even a bit menacing. She slid the cutlass back into its place at her waist and watched Po Tsai. He rolled his eyes and snapped at the men to get back to work.

"Greater pirate than Zhèng Yī?" Po Tsai retorted, turning his attention to Mógū.

"The greatest pirate in history to ever sail the south seas," she deadpanned. At that moment, she realized she would show the world what a woman could really accomplish, with or without Zhèng Yī and Po Tsai.

Chapter Thirteen – New Boots

For the rest of the day and all of the next one, Mógū walked around in her house slippers with the confidence of a commander. She assisted the others with the contents of the ship noting a few more items she felt were warranted; a bolt of fine white linen, a bolt of dark gray wool, a large spool of heavy taupe thread and several strips of dark brown leather. Together, she and Chūntáo would create an outfit for her with layers to accommodate the many temperature changes on the boats. She could envision it, the way it would fit and be slightly expandable for her body's inevitable change with pregnancy.

The second full moon was only a few days away. She had one more complete moon cycle before she would tell Zhèng Yī but, in the meantime, a looser tunic and belt would be more comfortable for her and would disguise any baby pudge her body may produce.

Towards the end of the second day, Mógū received a message from a lackey that the blacksmith requested her presence at her convenience.

"The blacksmith?" Po Tsai questioned, "what's that all about? A new chastity belt?" he chuckled and looked to the other men to back him with their own laughter. Some of them did with half-hearted guffaws.

"No, but that's an excellent idea, Po Tsai," she said and handed him the large ledger book. "Be sure that gets put back when you're done with it." They had been inventorying crates of wine and she was more than a little tipsy from sampling the long, narrow bottles.

Zhèng Yī had told Mógū she could have their brood mare, Mā, for the ride back and forth from the house to the harbor. Normally she didn't expect anything from the old girl but a reliable ride, but today she beckoned the horse to trot then run. The nag was lighter on her four feet than Mógū had expected. They both enjoyed the extra exertion and were to their destination in what seemed like mere moments.

The blacksmith handed the boots to Mógū without a word. She inspected them before taking off the now worn slippers and sliding her feet into them. They were magnificent. Another experience that exceeded her expectations today. The blacksmith had not put the nails through the heel as she had told him to but instead fashioned a new metal heel to the boot with dozens of sharp, short spikes. The front of the boot had also been modified with a rolled piece of metal to create the same height from front to back. The blacksmith watched her rocking back onto her heels then up onto her toes.

"It's so you don't get stuck," he offered without prompting. She nodded. He continued, "If the heels dig too far in the wood, you could get stuck but if you rock onto the front of the boot with your body weight, the heel will release."

The floor of his work space was dirt but Mógū could feel the play beneath her soles as to what he meant.

"You did fine work, thank you," she said respectfully, "I will have my lackey bring your compensation."

"Thank you for the opportunity to serve you, Madam Zhèng Yī," he replied with just the same amount of respect. "Be safe, there is no need to pay me. I am here to serve you," timidly he added, "We would all like to see the day that Zhèng Yī has a blood-born son. That is my blessing to you and him, my wish. Be well." He bowed respectfully then returned to his work table.

A fluttering in her stomach caused Mógū to instinctively put her hands across her belly. With some certainty, she suddenly knew the child was a boy. Moreover, she knew he would not terminate but be born healthy and grow to adulthood. The information flashed into her mind in an instant. *Yīngshí* his name came to her, *Zhèng Yīngshí* first born son to the great Zhèng Yī. Her heart swelled with love for her husband and this unborn child.

She looked at the man standing at his table, he was watching her, waiting for her to leave so he could continue his day. "Thank you, for the blessing and the boots. I will see what I can do." With a sly smile she turned and exited the blacksmith's quarters.

Chapter Fourteen – Training

The crew hadn't sailed in over two weeks and Mógū was anxious for this trip. In that half a month, she had transformed from wife of Zhèng Yī, to Madam Zhèng Yī, pirate. Chūntáo had used stiff leather that was usually reserved for saddle making to create a bodice for her. It covered her breasts and was cut higher in the front than back to accommodate her expanding stomach. It was stiff and would act as armor if necessary. Chūntáo had also created a new feminine warrior outfit with fine white silk and warm gray wool. For warmth, the wool was a lining inside the loose-fitting pantaloons. If Mógū was standing, the bottom of the outfit looked like proper Chinese *qipao* but when she moved, it was clearly pants.

Much to Po Tsai's chagrin, Zhèng Yī had been an encouraging husband when it came to the weapons. He had shown Mógū how to load the pistol and fire explaining what could go wrong if it was loaded incorrectly. It was a single shot, side hammer pistol most likely from Britain. He told her she only got one chance to use it so 'make it count.' They practiced firing it at old clothing that had been stuffed with straw and mounted to a post set a few paces away.

"You will not be able to reload during a raid so use your cutlass when you can and reserve that single shot for life or death emergencies," he explained as he showed her how to aim and fire. "You have exquisite taste in arms," he noted as he watched her fire the one loaded shot dead center into the stuffed dummy.

"And in husbands," she said with a warm smile as she turned to him and kissed him. She had been waiting for the perfect time to tell him of her pregnancy and thought this may be it when she heard horse hooves approaching.

"Here's the man of the hour," Zhèng Yī said as he pulled away from her and greeted Po Tsai. "I thought I could show you some sparring tricks and asked Po Tsai to join us for the lesson." His smile was warm and radiant. Even though she was a bit put out by Po Tsai's presence she was looking forward to the combat training the men would provide.

After a quick but informative lecture, the two men began to spar. Zhèng Yī offered direction as he moved and offset Po Tsai's aggressive form.

"Run him through!" Mógū exclaimed getting caught up in the mock sword fight. She saw Po Tsai's eyes dart towards her voice for an instant. Zhèng Yī took advantage of the moment and moved in, bringing his sword to Po Tsai's throat.

Zhèng Yī chuckled and gave Po Tsai a wink. "Well played patience and timing and you'll be victorious in every battle, my wife." He moved to her and lightly brushed her lips with his. "Are you ready to give a go?"

She sparred with Po Tsai for what seemed like an eternity. Her arms felt like limp noodles but eventually the cutlass became an extension of her body.

The following morning, as they set sail, Mógū's confidence heightened. She was certainly dressed the part and ready for whatever they may encounter.

Mógū took her place at the bow of the junk. She stomped one foot, then the other to drill the sharp heel into the wood. It was secure and she felt every bit the part of the pirate ready for battle. Keeping her knees soft and slightly bent, she felt her back stiffen and stood prominent knowing Po Tsai was watching her every move.

Around midday Mógū noticed a small ship on the horizon. Glancing around, she realized the fleet had already spotted it, their attention turned towards the small vessel. They were still sailing in a single line, but she knew as they approached, the rest of the fleet would spread out. She respected the military maneuver and what the psychological surprise of dozens of junks did to the boat they were pursuing.

When she turned her attention back to the boat in the distance, she realized it was not as small as she originally thought and there were three ships instead of one. As if in a coordinated dance, the three ships circled around and came together readying themselves for a battle. This was not the norm that she had experienced. On both prior outings, their junks had pursued their quarry until they could take it over. Neither had much of a fight.

Squinting her eyes, she tried to make out the flag that hung slack on the mast. Clearly, it was not British.

"Portuguese," Po Tsai answered her thoughts and startled her slightly when he approached. She had not expected him to leave his post. She realized all the fleet had slowed and the back boats were fanning out creating a long band of junks on the horizon. The wind gusted slightly and the flag moved so Mógū could see it in its entirety, shaped like a shield with a crown on the top it fluttered then fell back to its limp position.

"Maria's men," Po Tsai mumbled under his breath.

Glancing to the right, Mógū saw her husband standing on the bow of his junk, a brass telescope held to his eye. *All the best captains stand there*, she heard Po Tsai in her mind, perhaps he hadn't been trying to kill her on their first couple runs. After a moment, she realized everyone was watching Zhèng Yī, waiting for his command.

"They're cunning bastards," Po Tsai stated, his eyes trained on the ships in front of them, "those boats are all full of salt, you can see how they sit so low in the water. They have not made it to the trade harbor yet. There may be blacks too, but perhaps not."

"Black what?"

"People. You've never seen Africans before?" Mógū thought about it for a moment and recalled a regular on the flower boat whose skin was as dark as coffee, his hair tight and curled like dark, soft lamb's wool. She nodded absently and thought about humans as cargo. "The Portuguese don't hightail it, they'll fight. This is going to get ugly, are you sure you're up for it?" Mógū's attention returned to Po Tsai and she nodded. Simultaneously they turned their attention to Zhèng Yī who had put the telescope away and was glaring at their opponents. He made a signal with his hands and Po Tsai repeated it three times. She looked to the left and saw the other men repeating the motion. "The junks on the outside are going to circle in. From what I can tell, Zhèng Yī is going to surround them and we'll all move in at once."

This was it, her first real combat. Mógū's pulse raced as the exhilaration of the impending battle settled into her veins.

Chapter Fifteen – First Fight

Mógū held her blade close to her chest mimicking the pose Zhèng Yī was in. When he moved and signaled, she would do the same. Po Tsai's breathing had become a little more labored as he stood next to her and watched the three enemy ships. Their ships had come together forming a semi-circle. All their men stood at the ready as did Zhèng Yī's men. The tension on her boat was palpable.

She stared at Zhèng Yī waiting for his signal, glancing at the Portuguese ships every now and then. For some reason, it occurred to her she was the only woman in all three dozen vessels. It didn't matter though; she would fight like a man. She would kill. *Kill.* The word echoed in her brain as flashes of the last day on the flower boat flickered in her mind. She had killed a man that day too so she knew she could do it.

Her stomach flipped and she wondered if it were nerves or the baby wishing her luck. Knowing in her heart the revelation she had about the baby being born healthy gave her the comfort she needed to get through the moment. She knew she would come out of this alive and well enough to give birth to Zhèng Yī's first-born son. It gave her confidence and a strange sort of power she had never felt before.

The signal came. Zhèng Yī held his sword straight up and the ships seemed to all move at once. She mimicked the motion and noticed the others on the bows were all holding their swords high above their heads too. A loud boom brought her attention to the Portuguese boats. They had fired their cannon towards Zhèng Yī. He hadn't even flinched as it splashed into the water less than a rod away from the bow of his boat. Mógū had helped unload cannons from the two British ships but had never seen one fired. The boom came again, and again, and again. Musket and pistol shots could be heard from all sides too. She realized even though the Portuguese scoundrels were shooting at them they continued to edge forward.

There were a lot of men on those ships. With the British, there had only been a couple dozen. Their men had made it look so easy, but these boats had at least a hundred men each. They still out-numbered them, but this was a completely different fight.

She could see the junks circling up and around the three foreign boats as Zhèng Yī's boat made a sudden surge forward. Mógū glanced at the bow and saw Zhèng Yī was no longer standing on the bow. She knew he had climbed the mast so when they were close enough and his men began to board the opponent's ship, he would observe from a higher vantage point then swing down on a rope landing in the middle of the fray.

Her junk began to pick up speed. Zhèng Yī's was still leading but hers was closing the gap. The slap of the oars into the water in unison created a rhythm in her head. She bent her knees into a low crouch and pressed her heels deep into the wood preparing for the impact. Once they were close enough, Po Tsai would give a command and all the men on one side of the junk would stop paddling and hold their oars stiff in the water causing the junk to do a forty-five degree turn and slide parallel into the other ship. That way many men could go over the railing directly onto their adversaries' craft without getting in each other's way.

Before the ships collided, many men began jumping from railing to deck. Battle cries and painful groans rose in unison. The boats struck each other with a crack and from the corner of her eye, Mógū saw her husband swing down from a rope as their ship rocked limiting the distance of his drop. He landed with the grace of an acrobat.

Mógū watched as Zhèng Yī began to take down the Portuguese men. He held a dagger in each hand and she could see his pistol tucked into the uniform's waist wrap. His right arm swooped, ramming the blade into the back of one man as he pulled out the dagger from another's back with his left. The metallic smell of blood rose around her.

She rocked forward releasing her heels from being pressed into the deck. Her attention was drawn to a man in a white uniform. He was a pale shade of brown, and even with his naval hat, she could tell his hair was cropped short. In one hand, he held a cutlass similar to hers, in the other, a long, sharp sword. His entire uniform, face and hands were covered with blood. She watched him move closer to her, his cadence was similar to her husband's, stab, slice, stab, slice, all the while avoiding the back-swings of those fighting around him.

One of Zhèng Yī's men fell to his knees on the deck in front of the Portuguese man who kicked him brutally in the jaw then ran his sword through another of the pirates. Mógū rocked further forward to ensure her heels were free. Her heart raced as if she had been running, her breathing deliberate and deep. She looked over to Zhèng Yī who was still knifing every man within reach. It seemed he was surrounded. She turned her attention back to the tall Portuguese man who was now only a few yards away.

She wanted to run to Zhèng Yī, to help the unfair numbers against him but her gut told her she wouldn't make it unless she killed the man in the white uniform. She sprung up from where she had been crouched and leapt onto the railing holding her cutlass above her head with both hands. The man began to swing his cutlass upward at her as she plummeted towards him. Their eyes met and she saw a momentary flash of confusion in his expression. The sword in his right hand hesitated for a heartbeat, long enough for Mógū to swipe her blade across his neck. The confused look was still on his face as his severed head hit the deck.

Mógū turned her attention to Zhèng Yī in the boat next to where she stood. She could no longer see him. Panic swept over her like a heavy, dark wave when she caught a glimpse of his red tunic. He was engaged in battle with a larger man in a white uniform. Without thought, she pulled her pistol out from its hiding place, swung her arm up and fired in one fluid motion. The man's head snapped forward and then he fell back. With relief, Mógū saw Zhèng Yī pull his dagger from the now dead assailant.

She saw the look on his face register that he was no longer in immediate danger. His eyes darted to hers and he grinned a lop-sided, bloody smirk as she heard Po Tsai yell from behind her "Pòchān!" the command it was over. The two-syllable word began to spread as others repeated it for all to hear. Relief washed over Mógū, for a moment she thought she may need to vomit. Zhèng Yī moved from across the deck towards Mógū, a wide smile gracing his face.

They were victorious once again. Whoops and hollers of victory echoed across the decks of the ships as the wounded were attended to and the dead were rolled into the sea. The noise, the movement of the boats rocking into each other and the smell of death all of a sudden became too much for Mógū and she bent over at the waist and emptied her stomach.

"This is why we don't have women on the crew," Po Tsai said sarcastically to Zhèng Yī who had almost reached his wife. She raised her hand to him and hurled again. He stopped in his tracks. A look of concern had fallen across his face. "They can't handle the blood," Po Tsai continued.

She finished with a few dry heaves and stood up to face Zhèng Yī who had respectfully kept his distance of a couple yards.

"It's not me who cannot handle the smell of blood, but your son," she said proudly and flashed a full-toothed smile at her husband while simultaneously moving her hand to her belly.

"No!" Po Tsai snapped.

"Yes!" Zhèng Yī exclaimed and took long strides towards Mógū. He threw his arms around her and kissed her passionately.

"Yīngshí," she whispered into his ear.

His head bobbed on her shoulder, "Yes, yes," he breathed, "our son, Zhèng Yīngshí. Oh, Mógu, I couldn't be happier."

Even though happiness had been a foreign feeling most of her life, she couldn't have agreed more.

Chapter Sixteen – Fortune Loves Pig

The trip back was tense. As Po Tsai predicted, there were nine male Africans aboard. The pirates had taken them from their hold, and removed their shackles. They were no threat to any one of Zhèng Yī's men. Mógū had suggested getting them a meal since they clearly looked neglected.

Po Tsai's temper flared. "I'm not feeding their cargo with food that would be better served to my own crew."

"Their cargo? They are men! Where is your compassion?" Mógū argued back, "They're hungry and we have plenty."

Zhèng Yī chimed in, "Po Tsai, let's not upset my wife while she is in this delicate condition—"

Mógū cheeks blazed. "Delicate condition!? Did you not see me fight today? Was I not—"

"I was busy with my own battles," Zhèng Yī interrupted her. "Perhaps Po Tsai is right and this isn't a place for a lady."

"You didn't marry a lady, you married a partner. You married me. Let me remind you, half this fleet is mine."

"Having half the fleet on a contract and being here in the midst of the bloody fray is completely different and you know it." Zhèng Yī was resolved; he folded his arms across his chest and raised his eyes so he was looking over the top of Mógū's head.

"But that's not fair," she protested, "I'm a great warrior. I saved your life today. I could—" Zhèng Yī's jaw was set firm; he did not look at her.

"You got lucky," Po Tsai interjected.

"Because I *am* lucky! We have been victorious three of three times I've been a part of this crew, it is luck indeed. Zhèng Yī, please, I'm begging you."

"You are my wife and will do as I say." Zhèng Yī's voice was low and authoritarian. She paused, hurt by his tone.

"Yes, husband," she replied with bitterness.

Zhèng Yī had insisted Mógū not help the crew inventory and categorize the most recent booty. Much to her annoyance, he stated he wanted her to stay inside and not engage in anything too strenuous.

"Oh, you do what your husband tells you," Chūntáo chided after Mógū had told her the story. Chūntáo added her clothes to the still warm bath water to soak once Mógū got out. She then took the leather breast plate and began rubbing palm oil over it to blend the blood stains out

There was a soft knock on the large door. She knew it was Zhèng Yī. Mógū continued to work the knots from her wet hair with a large wooden comb. She was a bit irritated he had stopped by her chamber to make sure she had done as he instructed.

"The nine dark men have all agreed to join our fleet," Zhèng Yī stated, "I thought you would want to know." Mógū nodded and continued to work on her hair. She knew there wasn't a choice for the African men. They would join the fleet or be killed. *White men are so uncivilized*, she thought thinking of the human cargo, but the addition to the fleet would be warranted and welcomed. She wondered if they could fight once they had their good health back.

"This isn't a punishment," Zhèng Yī's words brought her back to the present. "It's to protect my son, it's for his safety that you don't fight. Once he is born, you can return to the junks." She saw a small grin playing at the corners of his mouth. "Will he be born in the year of the dog or pig?"

Mógū felt her resolve soften; she couldn't help but return the smile. The excitement of the baby was exuding from every pore of Zhèng Yī's face. "Black Water Pig," she announced.

"Fortune loves Pig," Zhèng Yī said, a smile lighting up his whole face, "he will be a great businessman, but peaceful, strong, persistent."

"Unless it's a girl," Chūntáo piped up from the divan where she was still cleaning Mógū's leather armor.

"It's not," Mógū and Zhèng Yī answered in unison. Chūntáo rolled her eyes. Zhèng Yī moved closer to Mógū, then lightly kissed the top of her still damp head.

"I'm so grateful you agreed to be my wife," he said softly into her ear.

The noise she produced was half laugh, half sob. She nodded her head and wrapped her arms around his waist. "Me too, husband. Me too."

Chapter Seventeen – Business Ventures

Mógū knew the pre-marital agreement verbatim. Even though half the fleet was hers, a man's ego could be a fragile thing. She had learned while working the flower boats how to make a golden situation appear to be the man's idea. Determined not to sit around and get fat while pregnant, she needed a plan to keep herself busy and make some money all while being what Zhèng Yī referred to as 'Yīngshí's safe and sound,' never contemplating the sex of the infant.

Mógū sat on large pillows on the floor of her room and readied a pipe of opium. Since she had been pregnant, she had to cut back on how much she smoked as it gave her a headache and left her nauseous. The blue pills in her tea were nice but nothing in comparison to smoking. If she only smoked one hit, she could curb her upset stomach with a dim sum of baked honey cake. As she exhaled, she laid back on the pillows and watched as the sunlight lit up the smoke, making it appear alive. It moved and danced above her as she closed her eyes and allowed the softening of her body as the drug consumed her.

In her vision she saw two women, sisters, riding elephants holding family crested shields that were bright yellow and blue. They beckoned for her and she rode the beast on top of the sea along a pristine shore. She marveled at how the elephants' feet skimmed the top of the water. It felt like she was flying. Occasionally she saw little fishing villages which made her wonder where her dreams were taking her. She watched as the shore continued taking in the people and boats. Finally, she realized it was Dai Nam or Annam as it was referred to centuries before.

As Mógū came to from her momentary kip she realized the two women were the famous Tru'ng sisters who ruled that area from the overshadowing Chinese early in the modern era. It was a sign. The money could be made from Dai Nam.

Nguyên Anh was recently in rule of this area organizing the next in line of multiple family dynasties. The long, narrow country ran north and south along Laos, Cambodia, and China. Even though it was a poor country, the access to the sea and harbors were invaluable. The French and Chinese were both interested in the country's resources and people. It was common knowledge the land was fertile and farmable.

Mógū suggested to Zhèng Yī that she take several dozen junks and create a shoreline presence in exchange for farm land as well as a protection tax paid by the newest royal heir. Zhèng Yī was amused and told her there was no way she would be able to talk Nguyên Anh into the financial aspect of her proposal.

"I can be very persuasive," she told him over late-night drinks in his chamber.

"Don't I know it." He laughed.

"It wouldn't make sense for him to say no," she said.

"Men sometimes don't do the things that make the most sense," he retorted.

It was her turn to chuckle. She knew it was true but the idea was firm in her head. The dream was the direction she sought, brought to her from beyond the grave by powerful women. "I'll present it to the emperor as a positive. It will alleviate his navy and men so they can be more resourceful and build the villages into bigger towns."

"I'm not sure Nguyên Anh has a formidable navy." Zhèng Yī pondered the discussion.

"Well, all the more reason to agree to the tax, it would be in their interest. The dynasty would never attack the beaches of Dai Nam with the presence of our men. Their little communities would be secure."

Zhèng Yī nodded. "I would feel better if you could take Po Tsai. Would you agree to that?" he asked without looking at her.

"I suppose," she replied suppressing a little grin.

It took them only a few days to coordinate and prepare for the journey. Zhèng Yī and Po Tsai worked together to be sure they had provisions for whatever may happen. When the time came, more than a hundred boats left in formation at dawn with her junk in the lead and Po Tsai's bringing up the rear.

Huê was the most recent capital of Dai Nam and the city where she would find Nguyên Anh. Located approximately mid-point in the country, where the north and south had come together, it was the largest municipal in the country. The harbor was built up and could accommodate several trade ships at once.

She had given the signal for the boats to line up a few furlongs from each other along the coast. Her boat, as well as five others, continued towards the port. Po Tsai would manage the boats left on sentry.

Mógū could see the activity of the town, the people doing their daily activities, selling their wares, fishing, tending to children. Many men were on the beach cleaning fish then spearing them with long bamboo sticks and placing them in a smoker that had been built out of clay. More men were on the docks than she guessed was normal, many dressed in some type of uniform. The crowd got bigger as they approached. A few of the villagers had rudimentary weapons in their hands. The uniformed men had swords at their waists, but she saw no guns. None of them would stand a chance against her crew, she could see in their faces they knew this to be a fact.

One of the men on her crew knew enough of the language that he was able to convey that Mógū, "their queen," wanted to speak to their leader, the honorable Nguyên Anh. *Queen* she mused, but really, what else would they have called her to open the line of communication with Nguyên Anh? 'Queen Zhèng.' She had to admit, it had a nice ring to it.

An image of her wedding day flashed in her mind, the way she was carried to the altar in her red dress. Perhaps she should have worn it instead of the warrior garb Chūntáo had made. *No*, she thought, the cutlass at her waist and the pistol tucked into her wrap was just as strong a visual presence as the expensive dress.

The interpreter had assured the fishermen there would be no blood shed as long as one of them could secure a meeting with their leader. A ripple of nervous energy moved through the throngs of people who had now gathered to see what was happening. Mógū glanced over her shoulder, her fleet held in formation up and down the coast as far as the eye could see, the red flags moved and danced in the breeze offering her silent encouragement and a sense of security. Zhèng Yī was right about sending Po Tsai, she felt poised and protected. A surge of power aligned her spine and filled her with the confidence she would need to negotiate a fair protection levy with the new emperor.

The logistics of what she was proposing twisted in her head. In her mind, it seemed like a two-stage win. Instead of sailing, chasing and ultimately hunting the trade ships, her thought was to line the fleet along the coast of Dai Nam. She would propose a charge to Nguyên Anh for their presence. Ships would pay to pass as well. From Korea to the Philippines there were plenty vessels moving from north to south daily. A small fee to pass without a fight would be reasonable, and if a ship happened to think they could take down one of her fleet, they would be defeated regardless of the country from which they came.

The trade ships would continue to come and go and would become easy pickings if they were set up strategically enough to intercept them without bringing attention from the Chinese. This was part of the tactic she would keep to herself, a financial bonus.

Her attention was brought back to the moment at hand as the gangplank was being secured for their exodus. Three of her men went before her and created a small arc at the dock end of the plank ensuring her safety as she descended. Once she was on their small dock, two additional men closed in behind her so she was shielded from all sides. They walked in formation for several furlongs where a half dozen men in uniform met them. The journey continued flanked with the men of Dai

Nam. Mógū let her eyes wander over the landscape as they walked, this land was green and lush. The rumors were right, it could be farmed, it was much more fertile earth than the island where they lived.

Eventually, the path turned to a road. The heavy tree line opened as they reached a large building made of stone and ascended the stairs. The military type men stayed outside. Mógū and her guards were told to wait while they informed Nguyên Anh of their arrival.

Chapter Eighteen – Nguyên Anh

It must have been something about the smell of the incense or the lighting of Nguyên Anh's great hall that gave Mógū a flashback of her youth to the day she was sold from the monastery to the flower boat. She had been thirteen, her first blood just passed when the nuns made the business transaction. It was no surprise. All the girls were sold to flower boats once they had become women; their virginity auctioned to the highest bidder. The nuns made money, the flower boat made money, everyone was happy if not the young lady whose fate had been delivered without contemplation.

"I don't know how to work on a flower boat," Mógū had told the head nun as they walked back to her shared room for her things.

"It's innate, comes natural," she mumbled without looking at Mógū, "men are simple creatures, you'll figure it out." The last sentence rang in Mógū's ears as she was properly introduced to Nguyên Anh.

They sat on the floor on a large ornately woven rug. The men flanking each of her sides. Nguyên Anh sat across from her with his own bodyguards. There were two interpreters and Mógū's man explained to her how the negotiations would work to keep the conversation flowing and fair. Each time one spoke to their leader, the other would have to give a physical verification the tête-à-tête was accurate before answering. Mógū agreed to the process and sat quietly until it was her turn to speak, playing the expected role of the woman, heeding the lessons from the nuns and her flower boat experiences.

When the proposal was laid out in his language, Nguyên Anh rolled back and laughed. A ripple of sniggers floated across his men's mouths. Mógū felt the energy of the room change as her men stiffened with indignation, their mood tense. She giggled like a child and cast her eyes down demurely like a proper lady. This act added the slightest air of confusion to all the men.

Once the laughter had stopped, she smiled warmly. "So that's a yes? For all terms?" she beamed. As the interpreter translated, she raised her eyes to meet Nguyên Anh's. His face had grown grave, he shook his head. "Tsk, tsk, you are such a wise man to agree so easily." She kept her voice light and friendly. "Very smart indeed."

"Why would I agree to these ludicrous terms presented to me by nothing but a lowly woman?" the interpreter spoke after Nguyên Anh. His jaw was set, his eyes bore into hers.

"I would think a smart man like yourself would want less problems, not more," she crooned, still smiling, "I know about your challenges with the Chinese. We are not loyal to the Dynasty, nor do we bow to the British, French or Portuguese." She took a sip of rice wine and let the interpreter catch up. "It seems to me you have your hands full. Simply compensating us to watch over your sea borders will alleviate some of those worries. Then, when your country is safe from Youngyan and his nasty men, you can concentrate on the civil disruption in your midst, bring Dai Nam together, stop the local rebels. The things most important for your people."

Nguyên Anh was confused but she could see the thought process in his expression. "What do you want? Specifically."

"Land for starters," Mógū answered. Her hands were crossed neatly across her knees, her face had a sweet expression. "We need fertile pasture land to grow food for our people. And of course, there are other things of value to a growing community such as ours; live-stock, bamboo, weapons, silver, even some of the French franc would be nice." He began to shake his head before the interpreter had finished. She felt her face grow hard, and allowed it to be seen in just her eyes, the smile stayed but became inauthentic. "Or," her tone had taken an edge too, "we will just take what we want and you will never be the ruler you were born to be. With due respect, don't be stupid."

When the interpreter finished, Nguyên Anh's face pinched and he leapt to his feet, a long dagger flashed from a sheath at his hip. He moved towards Mógū who didn't flinch. Her men were on their feet in an instant, blocking access to her. They scuffled back and forth, words thrown at each other neither could understand. The interpreters were also on their feet attempting to calm each other's rival. Mógū picked up her rice wine and downed it in one gulp and got to her feet.

She removed the pistol from its secure place in her waist cloth, double-checked to be sure the round was loaded and then bellowed, "Gentlemen!" She held the gun in front of her creating a clear shot to the emperor's head. "Nguyên Anh is an intelligent man. I believe he sees things our way, don't you, sir?" Their eyes met over the barrel of the gun. The men in the room seemed to be frozen, the air seemed to grow cold.

Not a sound was made for several seconds. Mógū inhaled deeply and drew the pistol's hammer back. It made a deep click that seemed to reverberated through the room.

"I suppose there is enough land to be shared," Nguyên Anh said, his face still hard.

"Yes, yes, there is plenty of everything to go around." She smiled and lowered the pistol. "The protection is also something a great leader like you deserves, peace of mind," she continued as she replaced the gun in the folds of her clothes.

Nguyên Anh nodded. "There is strength in numbers," he added. The interpreter spoke the last comment and Mógū felt her smile become genuine again.

"The gods smile down on us both today Emperor Nguyên Anh." She bowed towards him, adverting her eyes, quickly transforming back to the proper lady she knew he expected. She exhaled as quietly as she dared while not looking at him. The adrenaline was still surging through her body. It was a bold move. Zhèng Yī will be proud she thought. "I will have my people write up the official agreement while you decide where the best place for our property will be, somewhere with a view of the ocean would be lovely," she smiled. Nguyên Anh rolled his eyes and mumbled something and then stopped the interpreter from speaking with a hand gesture. She could see he was steaming angry. The emotion from him made her smile even wider. "We are looking forward to a long and prosperous venture with you and your people."

Mógū and her men turned to exit the building and walk back to the harbor. As they emerged from the shade of the structure, she noticed the view of the sea. From where she stood, she could see the dozens of red-flagged junks to the north and south. They appeared to be motionless but she knew the activity that was taking place on board, it was routine. From behind her she heard Nguyên Anh's sharp intake of breath as she realized he saw her armada too.

Chapter Nineteen – Best Blessings

"To my brilliant wife," Zhèng Yī shouted as he raised his glass in a toast to Mógū. They had spent the better part of the day going over a map of the ports of Dai Nam and imagining the taxation they were about to levy on the small country.

"From what I understand, she was brilliant," Po Tsai chimed in, raising his glass, "the whole trip, couldn't have gone better."

"Look at her, so brilliant, it's blinding," Chūntáo added, slamming her drink in one gulp and leaning it towards Po Tsai so he could refill it. "Good stuff," she choked.

"It will take approximately fourteen days to go from Lan Tao to Ha Long Bay," Mógū explained, "That will include eleven stops to collect taxes and do trades with the locals."

"Two fleets of sixty boats every other week," Zhèng Yī added, his statement directed towards Po Tsai. "This will provide a massive amount of money for our growing army. With numbers like that we would be able to overcome any trade ship for pillage as well as battle any naval ship that may come their way."

Po Tsai was nodding. "It's a good plan, let's not forget the passage fee as well."

"Brilliant," Chūntáo raised her glass again and drank it down again, "you're all blindingly brilliant," she slurred.

Mógū went back to Huê with the contracts and tentative schedules. Zhèng Yī accompanied her to sign the official documentation.

She relaxed and let him dote on her and her expanding belly. Chūntáo had made her a lovely blue gown for the meeting, complete with a broad belt to secure both the pistol and cutlass.

Zhèng Yī's presence allowed her to just be an observer of the arrangement she had orchestrated. It was a day to look pretty and observe. The agreement meeting went as well as could be expected. Neither Zhèng Yī nor Nguyên Anh challenged each other. It was clear the emperor had seen the wisdom of the deal.

Mógū went on the first run south getting off at each stop and meeting the local office-bearers. The people of Dai Nam were pleasant and eager to do business with her. The only other ship they saw was Chinese. It was clearly on its way out to trade in India. Mógū thought better of taxing it, her mind was on the task at hand.

She went every other trip for the first four months. The land that was deeded to her was both lush and spectacular. It was further south than Huê so the weather was better for crops. Rice fields tiered up an embankment where there was a beautiful view of the beach and ocean. This was where she oversaw the building of her new bamboo house.

On the sixth trip Mógū and Chūntáo decided to stay until after the baby was born. Zhèng Yī agreed to let Wu Jun accompany them to be the official mid-wife. He insisted Měiyīng stay and run the kitchen.

"Take Chūntáo too," he had said, "no need for her to stay and aggravate Po Tsai."

Chūntáo staying was never an option. Of course, her longest friend and closest family member would be there with her while she gave birth. *Men were so oblivious to the obvious.*

On previous trips, Mógū had acquired some fine teak furnishings for the new house and had the interior completely custom fit with fine silk and expensive art. It was lavish and comfortable, the ideal place to bring her son into the world.

Labor pains began on a cool spring morning. They came fast and hard leaving Mógū gritting her teeth until she could take it no more and screamed out. She was in so much pain, she wished Zhèng Yī were there to offer her support, but then she was glad he wasn't, as the pain threshold was almost too much to bear.

Chūntáo reminded her, "Ordinary women give birth every day and you are no ordinary woman."

Wu Jun's composed demeanor and familiarity with the birthing process seemed to bring a sense of calm to everyone around. She firmly gave Chūntáo orders throughout the day. After a while, her water broke and the pains came more frequently and much harder. Wu Jun had Mógū get on her hands and knees and instructed her it was almost time to push. She had Chūntáo get in the same position and face Mógū to talk her through the last of labor.

"AAAHHHH!!!" Mógū screamed into Chūntáo's face.

"Rrrrooaarrr!" Chūntáo bellowed back, the sound coming from deep within her stomach.

Mógū shook her head. "You're not amusing little sister," she grunted.

"Bear down," Wu Jun instructed.

"Sure, I am." Chūntáo laughed, and then began to howl like a dog accompanying Mógū's anguished cries.

"Again," Wu Jun's voice commanded and Chūntáo ramped it up.

"Yap, yap, yap!" Chūntáo barked at the top of her lungs.

"Not you, you idiot," Wu Jun snapped.

Mógū's stomach tightened as she laughed and cried out at the same time. She dropped the top half of her body to her elbows as Chūntáo took her hands. Chūntáo moved her face very close to Mógū's and whispered, "May your little black water pig be blessed with your bravery and Zhèng Yī's good looks. I love you, big sister."

Mógū rallied her strength and pushed again, arching her back into the pain. She felt the baby pass through her then heard Wu Jun's matronly voice, "Here, here young man, here, here."

Chūntáo moved so her eyes could meet Mógū's. "It's a boy," she said.

Mógū nodded. "I knew it. Tell Zhéng Yī we were right. Yīngshí, my son. I knew it all along." She collapsed into a heap and took several deep breaths resting before the after birth came.

Moments later, Mógū's heart melted when she was handed the small screeching human being. Immediately, she knew her life would never be the same as this little writhing thing gave her something to live for beyond anything she had ever felt. He was perfect in every way and found her breast without hesitation, latching on with gusto. Mógū felt the ancestors smiling down on them both.

What will it be, what will it be, an artist, a king, a warrior fighting? A chant from her childhood flashed into her mind as she wondered the future for her son. She contemplated him being Zhèng Yī's right-hand man, *papa's little pirate*. The thought left her feeling a bit antsy. *No, my love*, she thought, *you will be greater than the man before you, kinder, and smarter. Like your grandfather.* This thought left a sad smile on her face as she remembered her own dad.

"True to his birth sign," Chūntáo said, bringing Mógū back to the moment, "little piglet," she said nodding her head to the swaddled babe.

"Yes," Mógū smiled down at him noting his dark hair and swollen, newborn eyes. His tiny hand was splayed out on her breast. She had never seen anything so perfect.

"Oink, oink," Chūntáo whispered as she put her arm around Mógū's shoulders and got comfortable next to her, "good job, mama."

Mógū nodded. She was exhausted and laid her head against her friend, closing her eyes to rest while the baby suckled.

Zhèng Yī traveled the Dai Nam loop to collect the protection tax and stopped twice monthly. Sometimes he would stay two weeks until the fleet came around again. A regular schedule seemed to naturally ensue. Mógū was thrilled Zhèng Yī was capitalizing on it, using the arrangement for more than deliveries and trade deals. Some of the men had staked out their own land. They brought their families to the shores of Dai Nam as well. A little community grew from nothing and began to thrive.

Chūntáo set up her herb and root shop. She also traded opium blue beads to select affluent clients. Mógū pushed herself to enjoy the slow pace her life had taken since Yīngshí had been born. Motherhood didn't come as natural to her as she thought it might. Occasionally her thoughts flitted to her mother. Mógū had wondered if being naturally maternal was inherent or something she needed to learn and practice like combat. Chūntáo seemed more capable of being a good nurturing parent and Mógū didn't mind letting her step into that role.

It wasn't long before Mógū was pregnant again and Xióngshí was born almost two years to the day of his older brother. The pregnancy and labor almost the same, Wu Jun and Chūntáo were present. Měiyīng had come this time to care for Ying during the labor and birth.

The mundane routine of motherhood left Mógū feeling restless. Each time Zhèng Yī left to go back to the sea, her heart pulled in two, one half wanting to live the life of a pirate and the other wanting to raise her sons. Once her boys were weaned and walking, the pull of the sea was too much and she made arrangements with Chūntáo and Wu Jun to care for her children so she could join Zhèng Yī and Po Tsai back on the junks.

It wasn't much of a decision for Mógū to leave her sons with Chūntáo but rather an opening for her to return to the sea and the life of raiding. It's where she belonged, standing at the helm of a junk with the wind whipping her hair around her face. She felt free and powerful. Zhèng Yī had a small fleet of massive ships built during the two years they had been settling in Dai Nam. To Mógū they looked ten times bigger than the junk she was familiar with. Zhèng Yī was childlike in his exuberance to show her the features of the larger ship.

"You could live on it," he told her with a broad smile on his handsome face. "There's a hold for livestock, a place for a vegetable garden and plenty of storage for weapons and trade stock."

As she took in the new craft, she felt giddy with the new travel possibilities. With a vessel like this, they could go to Africa or Europe. Mógū noticed it wasn't as responsive in the water; it was clearly built for long distances. Even though she was still partial to the smaller more agile junks, she had to admit, these new vessels were lovely—huge, but lovely. Each was unique in the hideous masks carved and painted on the bows. This gave her comfort, certainly these ornate carvings would keep the bad spirits away and protect the crafts.

The costal route for the ships had become second nature for the crews. A trade, delivery and pick up routine had been established. It kept Dai Nam's people connected and made trading more convenient. Nguyên Anh had successfully taken over as leader of the new dynasty and avoided civil unrest within the elite families of the sovereign country. To commemorate the success, he renamed his country Viet Nam and established a new gold flag with a large red circle in the center and a blue border that looked like ocean waves.

Zhèng Yī continued to catch Mógū up on the things she had missed while taking care of the children.

"It's become too easy. Nothing short of a job to run up and down this coast and collect money, I might as well be a shopkeeper or a politician," Zhèng Yī droned, "It's time for an adventure, woman!" He scooped her up in his arms and kissed her. "Let's get the boys and sail around the world. We can rule these waters, let the Portuguese and Brits open their passageways for us to travel to new worlds. Think of the societies we will discover and the new foods to eat. Yīngshí and Xióngshí can learn to navigate the boat by the stars, they will learn new languages and—" She breathed in the scent of him as he chattered on. An open seas adventure with her man and boys sounded like the perfect next chapter in her life.

She got so wrapped up in Zhèng Yī's story she swooned at the idea and it stayed with her, getting bigger and clearer in her mind. That night they lay together in the captain's suite of the huge junk. It sailed smoother but slower than the smaller ones she was accustomed to. In fact, it felt completely different. Nothing like the raiding junks.

Mógū watched her husband sleep then looked around at the extravagance before she nodded off herself. *I'm the luckiest girl from Guangzhōu that has ever lived.*

In the dream, she was on the uppermost deck with her sons, the sun was shining and she could see Zhèng Yī piloting the large junk. Gulls flew overhead and their sorrowful cries caused her to look up. As soon as her focus was above her the sky darkened to pitch black. She felt a panic and her eyes searched for her children. The wails of the sea gulls became more feline, guttural. In a panic, she circled around to get her bearings. A tiger pounced from the sky somehow. It came at her, eyes wide and dilated, mouth open, sharp teeth—

She sucked in a breath as she sat up in the bed. Her heart was pounding and beads of sweat were forming under her arms and along her hairline. Mógū looked down at Zhèng Yī who was still in a deep sleep. *Just a bad dream*, she thought as she recollected the tiger's mouth. As her nerves calmed, she laid back down next to Zhèng Yī. He instinctively put his arm around her shoulders and pulled her to him. His body was warm and she was comforted by his touch. She lay awake the rest of the night, unable to fall asleep, the darkness and tiger haunting her thoughts.

Chapter Twenty-One – Dark and Stormy Night

The next morning, Mógū joined Zhèng Yī at the massive helm. With junk boats, they used a rear rudder as well as large rectangular sails with bamboo rods holding them stiff to maximize the winds. The smaller junks were in a formation all around them and the other five identical larger junks. They moved in the water somewhat silently, the waves slapping the hulls being the main noise that rose up in the early hours of the morning. As the sun crested the horizon, it reflected between the sea and clouds. The light danced golden across the water and pink across the sky.

Over morning tea, they had discussed the plan for the next few moon cycles. Down and back up, down and back up to collect the tax and inform their trading clients of their intentions. They would set Po Tsai up to continue the trades and command the fleet. Once they had done two rounds they would stop and check in on the boys and Chūntáo. Many of their men built their homes near the Zhèng family's. They took up local wives and created a little village of their own people. Not Chinese citizens necessarily but of Chinese descent and not from Viet Nam either but loyal and in love with their new motherland. It was a safe haven for them there, protected by the boarders of Nguyên's country, the Chinese couldn't pursue or prosecute.

The Chinese had been getting more and more aggressive since the Brits had been sniffing around Lantau Island. It seemed settlers from Europe were ever present and things at every port seemed to be changing in a novel direction. They knew where the waters were safe from the Qīng Dynasty and Jiaqing's reign. Once they knew their legacy would continue with Po Tsai's help, they could begin their plan for leaving, navigating the safest route to the European continent and then the Americas.

The first rotation went without a snag. Everyone seemed cooperative and eager for the change of command from Zhèng Yī to Cheung Po Tsai. They loaded their wares in Ha Long Bay making many sales and trades. The tax had been collected for the month and the weather seemed divine for that time of year. Bright blue skies peppered with lofty white clouds indicated gentle winds and easy navigation.

A smaller junk took Mógū back to the large ship. It hadn't taken her long to get used to the grandeur of the new craft. It was a solid craft that stood high in the water. Its luxurious cabins, grand galley and massive open deck space caused a sense of pride in Mógū.

Zhèng Yī was overseeing the barrels of rice and rice wine being loaded on another ship. The autumn air was crisp. Without warning, the winds changed directions. The air temperature dropped. The shift caused the sails to snap. Within a quarter hour, the sky looked ominous. Dark, heavy clouds rolled in so low, Mógū thought she could reach up and touch them.

As the men readied their ship, one of the quartermasters approached her. "Madam Zhèng Mógū, if I may?" Mógū nodded and he continued, "Captain Zhèng Yī has dispatched an order that we will go now. Cheung Po Tsai will lead the second group and he, Captain Zhèng Yī, will come in the last fleet once they have finished securing the food barrels." She nodded knowing there wasn't anything to say, there was no reason for them to be on the same junk all the time.

They exited Ha Long Bay, the last stop for this run, and began the journey south through the Gulf of Tonkin to then catch the undercurrent of the South Sea and eventually catch the east-west winds that would take them far from the shore before moving north. Mógū noticed some movement on the horizon and squinted to make it out; it looked like several little ships. She retrieved the spyglass and looked again. Definitely ships, Chinese ships she guessed by the colors of the sails and the way the boats sat low in the water. Mógū glanced at the darkening sky and thought the Chinese ships must be returning before a storm had a chance of brewing up. She gave the signal to take them into deep waters and the junk made a slight turn then began to pick up speed when the masts were turned to catch the wind full force.

She looked behind to see if Zhèng Yī's ships were moving out of the gulf and into the sea. The water was choppy and the boat bounced with heavy splashes making it difficult to focus. She watched the smaller junks cruising next to her and realized they were practically jumping from wave to wave, hitting hard on each swell. The sea had gotten dark. Large clouds blocked the setting sun. She was not able to see anything behind her except a vast darkness that seemed to be consuming the world around them.

Lightning flashed and illuminated her surroundings momentarily but left her feeling anxious once the darkness settled back over their ship. She knew by second nature what needed to be checked before she slept, everything was set for the night of sailing. The men were at their stations taking care of the big junk as it bobbed through the whitecaps. As she checked in with them, they reassured her everything would be fine. Mógū wasn't entirely convinced but there wasn't anything to be done but try to sleep.

She tossed and turned. Each time she felt she would finally doze, the boat slapped hard onto the water or a large boom of thunder would roil through her cabin. It was the rain that finally lulled her into slumber but it was also the sound of rain that woke her a few hours later. It came in torrents and didn't let up. Visibility was stifled because of the weather and made sailing difficult and slow. Mógū watched behind them as much as in front hoping to see Zhèng Yī's two large junks and accompanying smaller vessels but the clouds and fog prohibited it.

The rain became worse the farther north they traveled. The smaller junks had tightened up their formation to keep visibility between them. It rained all day, all through the night and all the next day. Mógū knew even as slow as they had been traveling, they had to be getting close to home. It never took three full days from Ha Long to Lantau.

Some of Po Tsai's men appeared to assist them once they finally arrived in the harbor. The ships were moored two dozen deep for them all to be safely secured. They were all soaked and freezing cold. Mógū heard Po Tsai's voice before she saw him, he was asking for Zhèng Yī. She heard one of the men tell him Zhèng Yī and his men were not too far behind them.

Chapter Twenty-Two – A Bad Feeling

Mógū paced up and down the long shore watching the blackness as the rain continued. Eventually, it got light but there was no hint of the sun due to the thick clouds that hung low over the water. She was exhausted, dizzy from lack of sleep and food.

A figure was walking towards her and her heart skipped a beat. *Zhèng Yī?* Just as quick, her mood sank as she watched the man's gait. It was Po Tsai. Once they stood side by side, he turned his attention to the sea.

"Did you see them leave the Ha Long harbor?" he asked. She nodded but continued to scan the horizon. "Did you see any other ships?"

The Chinese boats flashed in her mind, the ones that she had convinced herself were just coming in to avoid the storm. "There could have been some Chinese fishing—" she stopped short realizing the boats were not fishing boats but Qīng ships. She turned and looked at Po Tsai who was now staring at her.

"Have you been out here all night?" he asked, she nodded feeling a sting of tears behind her eyes and a lump forming in her throat. "You should go get something to eat and rest, sleep a little." The tears welled in her eyes, a few drops spilling down her cheek. She shook her head and willed Zhèng Yī's junk to appear through the fog. "I'll stay down here," Po Tsai added, "I'll come get you as soon as he gets in." He was being serious she realized as her stomach growled with hunger.

"Promise to come get me?" she asked.

Po Tsai turned to her. "Yes." He nodded and made a little bow to her. "Now go and rest, it was a long trip."

Mógū finally relinquished and started walking away, back towards the grand house. Her heart seemed to be breaking. A bad feeling descended with the shower from the sky, her clothes suddenly felt heavy. She became aware of how soaked she was, each step seemed more difficult with the weight of the water pressing down.

Měiyīng was the first to see her as she came in to the big hallway. Mógū was grateful to the girl who rushed over to her and began to help her peel off the soaked layers of clothes.

"Go up to your room, I'll bring you some soup," Měiyīng said once the first layer of Mógū's garb was stripped off, "would you like an egg in it?" Mógū nodded and staggered towards her room.

It seemed a colossal effort to remove the rest of her clothes and get her night wear on. She wished Chūntáo was there. This is the time she needed her best friend's presence, and her children. She needed the distraction from the reality of Zhèng Yǐ's missing ships. Měiyīng rapped lightly on the door. She entered before Mógū had verbally answered. Měiyīng was carrying a tray. A large bowl of beef broth with steamed greens and a chamomile tea was placed in front of Mógū.

"Thank you," she told Měiyīng and poured a cup of tea. Once her stomach was full, she was able to drift into a fitful sleep.

Many hours later she woke with a start. The sun was deep in the western sky. She ran from her room to Po Tsai's room, it was empty.

Zhèng Yǐ's was too. She dashed out of the house and ran back to the harbor. Po Tsai was still there. He was sitting on a rock a yard up off the beach scanning the sea. A spy glass hung from his waist.

"Po Tsai, no!" she heaved.

"Let's not write him off yet," Po Tsai said, his tone flat and tired. "It's possible the storm blew them off course and they are more than a day behind."

She saw the glimmer of hope dim as their eyes met in the dusk, she nodded even though her gut told her something was wrong, deadly wrong.

Chapter Twenty-Three – A Hero's Farewell

After two more days of worrying and pacing, Mógū had to face the fact that Zhèng Yī was not returning. Po Tsai was tight-lipped and uneasy. It dawned on her he was feeling as bleak about Zhèng Yī's fate as she was.

Several more days passed with Mógū trading places with Po Tsai in the lookout spot still hoping to see the return of Zhèng Yī's ships. One morning, one of Mógū's crew approached her, his face was ghostly white and his eyes red-rimmed. He told her they had received word that the Chinese navy had taken down several of Zhèng Yī's ships. Mógū felt her face fold into a scowl as she waited for the rest of the news.

"Captain Zhèng Yī's ship was heavily damaged," he reported, emotion welling in his face. "We are to assume the storm finished it off."

Mógū blinked twice as she processed this news. What was he saying? That Zhèng Yī was alive? Or that he went down with his ship?

"I'm sure the captain stayed with his ship to the bitter end," the man answered her thoughts as a full-blown sob escaped his lips.

"Leave me," she said with sullenness, her eyes closed and she took in a deep breath. She listened as his footsteps receded then she opened her eyes and released the air in her lungs in a loud sigh. She continued to scan the horizon. The reality of what the messenger had told her enveloped her like a shroud, heavy, sad. She wanted her sons, she wanted Chūntáo. This couldn't be happening, not now that she had finally found happiness, now she had finally found love with Zhèng Yī. Did the gods hate her? Why would they give her gifts of family and love only to take it?

It started to rain again; the weather had barely let up in the week since they had returned from Dai Nam. The wet soaked into her clothes and hair, she squinted through the downpour and willed Zhèng Yī to appear on the horizon. With every fiber of her being, she willed his boat to sail up to the docks. She pictured him, handsome with that broad smile and dancing eyes. What she wouldn't give to hear his laugh, to feel his arms around her and—

Footsteps approached from behind and she recognized them as the graceful gait of Po Tsai. "Come now," he said gently, "it won't do any good if you stay out here and catch your death of cold."

"I want my husband."

"We all do," he said sadly, "but what we must admit is he is he is not coming back." Mógū shook her head as she continued to scan the horizon, it blurred from her tears and the storm. Po Tsai put his arm around her shoulders. She jerked away with a sense of violence.

"No, I will not admit it," she cried tears mixing with the rain as it poured down her face.

"You don't have to admit it," he replied, "it will be declared for you."

She turned and searched his face. She saw the pain in his eyes and knew he hurt at this devastating news.

"I want my sons," she sobbed.

"We've sent for them, they will arrive when the storm breaks."

"And Chūntáo."

"Of course," he said with bitter sarcasm, "I'm sure she will accompany them. We've also sent word to Zhèng Yī's brothers and father. They are planning a hero's memorial."

At that last word, Mógū's life crashed down and she folded her body in half and wept. Po Tsai lowered himself to the ground. She felt his presence and knew he was crying too. This was unfair of the gods. Unfair to her and her children. As an afterthought, she included Po Tsai in the list of those injured by this unfortunate twist of events. Unfair.

The following week was a blur. Mógū didn't seem attached to her body as preparations were made for the memorial service. Her sons arrived with a consoling Chūntáo who took charge almost immediately after disembarking. It was nice to have someone telling her what to do and making decisions about the mundane activities of the life that continued.

Before she knew it, they were at the Zhèng family temple where Zhèng Yī's ancestors were honored and worshipped. Their presence was a given; this is where the family came to pray to the ancestors for their wishes to be taken to the gods. The connection between life and death was essential. This sacred place was the only place that the family would gather to honor her husband. A shrine would be elaborately decorated to ensure Zhèng Yī had everything he needed in the next life. A bronze vessel full of wine had been inscribed with a respectful farewell. Another smaller pitcher sat next to the wine. Mógū knew the blood of a goat was coagulating in it. It was an appropriate offering to their gods. She knew there would be a feast later, hopefully by then, her appetite would have returned.

Mógū was dressed in the widow's wear, all white with a head piece that rivaled her wedding crown. Her sons were also dressed all in white. The youngest was irritated he couldn't run and play, his older brother scolding him as the unsympathetic disciplinarian he had grown into. *He will make a fine leader*, Mógū thought of her oldest child, *he will lead many armies into battle and be victorious.*

A flash of Zhèng Yī drowning in the cold sea snapped her from her reverie. *NO! I will protect him from that life, he will grow fat with many wives and children at his feet, never having to battle, never having to draw blood from his enemies.* This was her resolve. She would see to it that her boys would have everything they ever desired or wanted so they would never know life on the open sea; would never spill the blood of their enemies. A sorrowful tune began on a stringed instrument. It brought her back to the present, the noise sounded like a foreign language.

Mógū looked around her, many people had come to pay their respects. She and her sons sat receiving guest after guest long after the ceremony was complete. When Zhèng Sì, Zhèng Yī's brother and his family appeared, Mógū felt the tears renew.

"I want vengeance," she told Zhèng Sì.

"From the weather? From the sea?" he hugged her sympathetically.

"From the Qīng dynasty, they did this to him," she said through gritted teeth. He nodded and pacified her with another hug then moved his attention to Po Tsai as his wife approached the children with her children, their first cousins.

"I understand your pain," she whispered in Mógū's ear.

Mógū wanted to slap her sister-in-law across the face! She could not know this pain; her husband was here, alive. She bit her lip and stayed silent. "San wants to avoid Zhèng Yī's fate, he no longer wants his fleet. His wife confessed this to me when we received the news of—" Her words clipped the last of the unspoken sentence. "Perhaps you and the man-child could take over those ships," —her eyes flitted to Po Tsai who was still talking with Zhèng Sì— "it would double the size of your fleet," she continued, "and all of those men could continue work. I can't imagine them wanting to become farmers after the life they have lived. I would be grateful if Zhèng Sì quit too. It's too dangerous now days. I never want to be in your shoes, my sister."

Mógū nodded and realized her sister-in-law meant no ill-will.

As more family and friends came and went, Mógū's mind was spinning with the possibilities of acquiring San's fleet and joining forces with Zhèng Sì. With a fleet that size, they would be invincible.

During the mourning days where Mógū had to stay in, she spoke to Chūntáo about becoming the captain of the largest fleet in the south seas.

"You make me laugh," Chūntáo joked as she served Mógū her midday meal, "You're a woman, did you forget? Maybe you're hiding something from me in those britches." She laughed and took a long, pointed look at Mógū's crotch.

"I may be a woman, but I am a warrior too," Mógū answered taking a piece of the dim sum that was on the plate.

"Well, I know that, and Zhèng Yī knew that, Po Tsai may even have an idea of that but the rest of the world…"

The silence between them was heavy with the unspoken words. Chūntáo popped a piece of dim sum into her mouth and changed her tone as she spoke through the food, "You'll have to marry for anyone to take you seriously, like it or not, those are the rules."

"I'll not get married again," Mógū sighed, "I really had grown accustomed to Zhèng Yī. It could never be the same."

"Naturally, it wouldn't be," Chūntáo helped herself to more of Mógū's lunch. "I mean, I guess you could marry Po Tsai, then everything would basically stay the same."

Mógū's knee jerk reaction was to shake her head and say, "Eww, no."

"Why not? You stubborn ninny," Chūntáo said with a giggle, "You want to marry for love instead of power?" Her snicker had turned into a full-on laugh. "Love instead of wealth?"

"Stop laughing at me," Mógū protested as her own smile played across her mouth.

"Stop being a willful woman," Chūntáo countered.

As they finished their meal Mógū's head spun with the possibilities. Maybe Chūntáo was onto something. Marry Cheung Po Tsai, acquire Zhèng San's fleet, join forces with Zhèng Sì and become the wealthiest woman in all of China.

In all of the world.

Chapter Twenty-Four – Family Time

Life moved forward mixed with tears and throbbing at Mógū's temples. By the time the rains began to subside, the moon had grown fat and disappeared more than once. Had it really been two months since Zhèng Yī had been gone? Time seemed to be playing tricks on her. The days drug on in shrouded sadness, yet the months seemed to fly by. There was a mandatory period of mourning which would last no less than six months before she could even consider taking another husband. She knew it would take longer than that for her heart to heal but for her livelihood, she would have to remarry sooner than later. Now she had given it a great amount of thought, Po Tsai was the only logical option.

Between them, she and Chūntáo had contrived a plan that began with convincing Po Tsai the best option was for them to get married. He was the next in command and the legal heir to Zhèng Yī's fleet whether she wanted to admit it or not; hence her marriage in the first place. She kept curious without overly prying on Po Tsai's comings and goings and counted the weeks to when she could comfortably approach him about their union.

In the meantime, she visited her brothers-in-law and their families, bringing her young sons to bond with their cousins, listening to their wives complain about their husbands' long absences and in general getting a feeling of where each of them stood in relation to her and Zhèng Yī's fleet. It would be imperative for her to be able to convince them coming together in one large squadron would be beneficial to everyone.

She learned the rumor was true, San wanted to leave the life of being a pirate. Mógū got the distinct feeling Zhèng Sì was satisfied with the way things were and just assumed Po Tsai would take over Zhèng Yī's fleet.

One night while visiting Zhèng Sì and his family, Mógū found herself alone with her brother-in-law while his wife cleaned up after dinner and the children played in the candlelit yard.

"Why did all you boys sail under different colored flags?" she asked while sipping the after-dinner rice wine.

Zhèng Si's face softened as he took in the question. "Newly found testosterone, I suppose," he chuckled. He downed his rice wine in one gulp and poured himself some more, then held the flask out to Mógū. She held her cup out to be refilled. "I think it was partially our father and uncle's doing." Mógū felt her face twist into a question. "Well, it's as if by age my brothers and cousins were each given a few ships and a small crew. Our dads wanted to explore farther but needed a presence where they had already reigned. I think they wanted us to feel ownership of sorts, learn leadership and take charge. If they pitted us against each other, drew territory lines, we wouldn't ever get too big for them to manage." He paused and Mógū stayed quiet thinking there may be more to his story but after several seconds of silence she realized he was done sharing.

"Crazy how things change," she said softly and sipped the bitter liquid in her cup.

Zhèng Sì nodded. "San doesn't even want to sail anymore," he said with a slight shake of his head. Mógū forced a surprise look across her face, no need to show her hand. "It's true," Zhèng Sì continued.

Mógū made a tsk-tsk noise and finished her drink then held the cup out for another refill. "I can't wait to sail again," she said, "I love it, it's in my blood."

Zhèng Sì filled both cups and downed his in one gulp. "You're a rare find," he sputtered as his wife entered the room and joined them for another drink.

Mógū divided her time between San, Zhèng Sì and her own house during her mourning period. While home she kept her eye on Po Tsai, and while gone she had Měiyīng and Wu Jun keep track of Po Tsai's activities.

She validated San when he finally confessed to her he wanted nothing more to do with the pirate life.

"Legal fleets are getting too big and powerful," he told her, "the English fleets are protected by the Queen and the Portuguese pirates don't even pretend they are noble, they plunder under Clément's name without shame, the rat bastard! John VI will never take us. No, I will not serve under any crown yet we are too small to be independent."

Mógū listened with rapt attention even though she disagreed. When she found herself alone with Zhèng Sì a few weeks later, she gave her opinion highlighted with San's concerns.

"It's believed that if we sail, we'll be running under Qīng's flag," she said to her brother-in-law.

"No!" he nearly shouted, "little brother says that, but he's wrong." Mógū was relieved the two brothers had already had this conversation. "Do you believe you represent the Dynasty?"

"Absolutely not!" she snapped, "My loyalty is to Zhèng Yī and his family, my family, our sons." She let the last declaration settle then suggested they all fly under one flag. "It's the most rational defense *and* offense," she shrugged, nonchalant. "Imagine the brothers' fleets united against any crown fleet out there," she said softly, "we'd be unbeatable. The English ships are big and slow, those bastards are cowardly and we out-number mad Maria's fleet three to one," She could see in his eyes he was grasping the possibilities. She continued, "Po Tsai is a good captain, we could double the red flag fleet with ease and—"

"We should come together under one color in Zhèng Yī's memory, this would honor all the ancestors," he said. Zhèng Sì's eyes had glazed over slightly. "The flags should all be red."

"Yes," she breathed, "San could step down and farm with our people."

"That's noble," he agreed still lost in his own thoughts.

"Yes, noble," she said and poured them more rice wine. "If only I were married to a captain, I could also command a fleet. Po Tsai is a good leader but if we join forces with you and San, we may need more superior officers, especially if San steps down. Tis a shame you and little brother are already married."

She let her words drift and settle in the quiet room as she watched her brother-in-law process what was laid before him. Her skin prickled and she thought of a cat, poised and ready to spring, waiting for the precise moment of rodent execution.

"You have sailed with Po Tsai," he mumbled, still lost in a hazy rice wine induced thought.

"Many times," she replied quietly, the tension in her chest building as if the air in the room was being sucked out.

"Cheung Po Tsai is an odd duck." Zhèng Sì turned his eyes to meet Mógū's. She shrugged as if she had never noticed any oddities in her late-husband's lover. "If there were to be a union between you and him it would be for the better good of the entire family, the fleet and…" She had begun to nod a little, then more and more as the idea fully formed on Zhèng Sì's lips. "Yes, it's a good idea, a marriage between Zhèng Yǐ's wife and right-hand man, bringing the family under the red flags." Air returned to Mógū's lungs; she felt a wave of relief. Zhèng Sì continued, "This would be a great honor to my brother and all the ancestors before us, yes, yes." He drained his cup and locked eyes with Mógū who had taken on a curious yet indifferent look. "I will arrange it, the unification of Po Tsai and you. Together we will announce to San so he can retire to his rice fields and enjoy his children and the quiet life."

"You are so wise," Mógū said. She lowered her eyes as respectful women did when conversing with men who have the illusion of power. "I am but a humble widow ready to do what I can to serve my family." She poured another round of the rice wine and held up the glass for a toast. "To Zhèng Yī and the red flag fleet."

Zhèng Sì raised his glass. "To the red flag fleet."

Chapter Twenty-Five – Warrior at Heart

"Oh, you're good!" Chūntáo exclaimed after Mógū explained how she had laid the plan out to marry Po Tsai, "Beats having to get him drunk and making it *his* idea." She laughed. "Your idea worked much better."

Mógū was spending time with her sons and Chūntáo, getting ready for the impending departure of the fleet the next morning. She cleaned her leather breast plate, then her boots. Chūntáo was letting out the hem of Yīngshí's pants as he hopped around the room in mock battle. His little brother toddled after him imitating the exaggerated moves the best he could.

Without warning, the door opened and a wild-eyed Po Tsai stepped into the room. "You are a widow in mourning!" he bellowed. Mógū's stomach turned with anxiety. *What was he talking about?* She had only been home from Zhèng Sì's house one day and one night, certainly the suggestion of marital ties wouldn't have come via a messenger. Mógū exchanged a confused look with Chūntáo.

Po Tsai pointed to the battle wear. "No."

"Are you drunk?" She stood and glared at Po Tsai. "Who are you to be telling me what I can and can't do?" Po Tsai's nostrils flared and his eyes shifted to the children who had frozen as if under a spell, then flickered back to Mógū's, she continued, "Are you suggesting that if I had died and Zhèng Yī was still here, he would sit around and mope for six months? You're out of your mind. I'm going." She turned away from him and continued to polish the leather of her breastplate even though it already shone as if it were new.

"But I, we—" Po Tsai stumbled on his words. His choppy lilt suggested he had been indulging in some rum or opium.

Chūntáo interrupted, "It makes no sense to constrain a spider from making a web and feasting on flies, why would you not want Mógū to join as a warrior if not commanding her own ship?"

"She's a woman," he answered flatly with a little confusion cresting his mouth.

"So is the spider that eats the flies," Yīngshí's childish voice piped up from across the room. The two women exchanged a worried look before Po Tsai began to chuckle.

"You are wise like your father, little man," Po Tsai said with a shake of his head.

"Did Zhèng Sì send a messenger?" Mógū asked.

"No, about?" Po Tsai's face had a look of concern. "You were just with him, were you not? Why would he send a messenger to me and not just send a message with you?"

Mógū shrugged. "I'm sure he's expecting me to go tomorrow with the fleet."

"Why would he?" Po Tsai asked.

"Well if you ask me," Chūntáo interjected, "it would be because she is a warrior at heart, able to command a ship of testosterone and still kill with the best of—"

"Oh, who cares what you have to say?" Po Tsai retorted. He stomped out of the room with Chūntáo on his heels.

"I hadn't even begun to point out the amazing mind this woman has. Much more than the average woman; quite a catch this one is."

Chūntáo caught the door so it didn't slam as Po Tsai exited. When Mógū and Chūntáo's eyes met, they both began to laugh. The boys followed suit as peals of giggles erupted from them all.

Before dawn the next morning, Mógū was up and dressed with an excitement she hadn't felt in months. She loved the open water, the chase of the ships, the fight and the best part, the victory. This would be the first raid she would go on without Zhèng Yī. A pang of loss jolted through her already racing heart as her emotions conflicted in her chest.

The horses had been brought from the stables by the lackeys. Hers was saddled and tied with Po Tsai's. Another horse was tethered to a cart full of food supplies. Mógū watched as Měiyīng secured the provisions then went back to the house for more. Měiyīng nodded her head towards Mógū as they passed each other. Chūntáo appeared in the doorway moments after Měiyīng went in. She appeared disheveled as if she had just woken. Yīngshí and Xióngshí appeared, following close behind.

"They wanted to help," Chūntáo mumbled.

"You two should be sleeping," Mógū cajoled.

"We want to be pirates too," Xióngshí said, his voice a little whiny. Yīngshí nodded his agreement.

Chūntáo shook her head and rolled her eyes as she picked up the boys and placed them on top of a large sack of rice in the food cart. "We'll ride with you to the harbor and say our goodbyes there." She climbed up into the front of the cart and made herself comfortable as the driver looked on a little startled. A commotion startled all of them as they watched Po Tsai appear and begin to shout commands. He glared at Chūntáo and the kids but didn't speak, Mógū offered him her most congenial smile.

"Good morning, Po Tsai," she said as he mounted his horse and jerked the reins to move away from them. Mógū shook her head as she watched him take the lead. The other horses and carts began to jerk forward and created a line down the path towards the harbor.

The sun crested the horizon, creating a slight yellow light in the distance. Mógū's horse had trotted up next to Po Tsai's. The horse-drawn carts were behind them and several dozen men on foot followed the carts. Mógū stared into the rising sun noticing the horizon wasn't smooth and flawless as it should have been. The path dipped behind the trees for a moment and obscured the view. Mógū prodded her horse to move ahead of Po Tsai's. He dug his heels into his horse's sides and it shot forward keeping the lead. Mógū leaned low and clicked her tongue to make a noise in the horse's ear and it ran forward passing Po Tsai. Mógū didn't look back as the horse darted down the dirt path into the clearing where the ships were docked knowing the competitive Po Tsai was right behind. She pulled her reins to slow and stop her horse as Po Tsai rode up next to her, the look on his face was as astonished as hers. The sight was magnificent. Their ships were tethered where they had been left the night before but dotted behind them, silhouetted by the rising sun, was thousands of junks. Due to the brightness coming from the east, it was not possible to distinguish the color of the flags, they all looked the same. She closed her eyes and they were all red behind her lids.

"What the—" Po Tsai began, Mógū cut him off.

"Zhèng Yī's legacy," she said a smile on her lips.

The food cart clambered behind them then passed to continue to the loading docks. "Mommy, look!" Mógū thought Xióngshí was pointing to all of the ships and didn't take her eyes off the horizon until she heard her son cry out, "Uncle Zhèng Sì!" he tried to jump from the cart but Chūntáo was quicker and secured him next to her. Yīngshí climbed over the buckboard and settled on her lap. Zhèng Sì was walking towards their small party, he waved his arm above his head and shouted to the children.

"What are they doing here?" Po Tsai asked, Mógū shrugged and dismounted.

"Good morning, brother-in-law," she called. The cart with Chūntáo and the boys came to a stop and they hustled down and ran to their uncle inquiring about their cousins.

"You are all too young to ride with us." He laughed and mussed Xióngshí's hair. "Soon though, you'll see, very soon then you'll wish you were still children and want to stay behind." He laughed and greeted Mógū.

"Why are you here?" Po Tsai asked still on his horse.

"And good morning to you too," Zhèng Sì continued to grin at them all. Mógū dismounted and started towards her brother-in-law.

"Really, why are you here?" Po Tsai's voice was stern and menacing.

"An alliance," he answered, "a joining of forces." He swept his hand towards the horizon where the multitude of ships sat bobbing in the early morning sunlight, "With a navy like that, we are unstoppable, don't you think?" Mógū watched Po Tsai's eyes scan over the fleet thinking the comment from Zhèng Sì sounded quite a bit like Zhèng Yī. She wondered if Po Tsai had noticed too.

"Certainly, these aren't all yours..." Po Tsai commented.

"San has decided to hang it up, he wants to be a farmer."

"I never understood the draw of the land," Po Tsai said keeping his eyes trained on the illicit navy.

"Ah, to each his own," Zhèng Sì threw his arm around Mógū and continued, "with a woman like this, Cheung Po Tsai, you would have it all, a wife and the sea. The best of both worlds."

"A woman like what?" Po Tsai asked, his attention snapping to Zhèng Sì and Mógū.

"A warrior, a leader, a beauty and a mother of my nephews. Why would you not want to marry Mógū?"

"Marry Mógū?" Po Tsai guffawed, "why would I marry Mógū? I don't love her." He flicked the reins for his horse who began to move towards the loading dock.

"A wise man once told me love is overrated," she called to his back. Po Tsai wheeled his horse around and circled back towards her and Zhèng Sì.

"So, this is what it's all about? A marriage proposal?"

"All what?" she asked perplexed.

"Zhèng Sì's show of power in front of your sons, this humongous spectacle of the ships, all of it, I just don't get it?" He slid off his horse and faced them.

"What's not to get?" Zhèng Sì asked with a smirk, "a marriage between you and Mógū would unite our families once again."

"You, Zhèng Yī's brother, feels he can speak for what's best for our families? Mógū is my... is my..." he stumbled on his words, "my mother."

"In title only Po Tsai the kid, in title only!" Zhèng Sì roared with laughter. Mógū couldn't help but smile, the chuckles were contagious. "It would be an easy process to renege, just a matter of formality really."

Mógū looked between Po Tsai and Zhèng Sì expectantly. After a few heartbeats, Po Tsai's features softened and Zhèng Sì's laughter subsided.

"I suppose," Po Tsai began, "what's in it for me?"

"What do you mean?" Mógū asked.

"A wife," Zhèng Sì piped in.

"I mean, as a woman, a marriage would mean you could have a voice, a career with the junks a future, but I'm being deadly serious when I ask, what's in it for me?" his eyes narrowed as he glared at them.

Mógū's cheeks flushed, this wasn't the answer she expected. Zhèng Sì stepped in, "You get to continue the life you have, Po Tsai. If you don't marry Mógū and she finds another husband, Yīngshí becomes Zhèng Yǐ's legal heir with Xióngshí in line behind him."

"That's not the way it works," Po Tsai chortled.

"It is when you have the family connections I have." Mógū saw Zhèng Sì's posture straighten with newfound confidence.

"It's like you told me all those months ago, think about the advantages of marrying into this powerful family." She searched his eyes steeling her own emotions. He was right, she needed this to happen, it would benefit her more than him.

"Fine," he said after what seemed like a very long moment, "raid with us this season and finish your mourning period. We can be married in the spring."

She nodded and mumbled, "Superb idea, Cheung Po Tsai, glad you thought of it." Her eyes met Zhèng Sì's and he winked at her.

"Now we have that settled," Zhèng Sì said to Cheung Po Tsai, "we are at your service. United we are unstoppable." He reached out and put his hand on Po Tsai's shoulder. "Welcome to the family."

Chapter Twenty-Six – Battle of Tiger's Mouth – 1809

Zhèng Sì had been right, with a fleet three times the size of Zhèng Yǐ's the Red Flag Fleet was a force to be compared to a weather phenomenon. Like a tsunami or hurricane, when the fleet sailed upon their prey, the fight was usually over quick.

With the British who fought with a regimented force, they were a predictable and tedious foe. Their ships were usually loaded with Chinese tea, silver and a lot of weaponry; specifically, cannons and rifles. That's where the Royal navy was easily defeated. The weapons had one shot then needed to be reloaded with gunpowder and another lead ball. Because of that, there seemed to be a pattern of where the gunfire would come from. This enabled Mógū's fleet to surround and advance with precision.

Mógū remembered Zhèng Yǐ once telling her it wasn't King George's navy to fear but the pirates who sailed protected by Queen Elizabeth.

"Their flag is black with a white skull, and crossed bones," he had told her, "their ships are as big as ours, and fast. It's wiser to avoid them."

All these months, and she had never seen one. Mógū suspected now England had banned the slave trade their lawless fleets were sailing in other oceans. Again, she recalled the tender moments between her and Zhèng Yǐ when they talked about traveling to other worlds that had been nothing but promising rumors to her; those hopes of raising their sons on the open water, exploring, pillaging, conquering, were over.

Her sons' sweet faces appeared in her thoughts. They were getting so big but still so small and fragile. She was glad they were safe with Chūntáo. This was no place for two small children. Most of their battles were much more difficult than the Royal Navy. The Portuguese, for example, were an entirely different challenge than the Brits. They fought with a ferociousness not seen in other navies. She felt they fought a bit underhanded but then again, she only recognized their devious battle tactics because she fought the same way, deliberately taking the opposing ships without damaging them to increase their own numbers.

The biggest problem with the Portuguese was their cargo ships were usually a one-time use coming from Africa with hundreds of dark-skinned humans that were sold as slaves. England no longer traded in slaves and the Chinese never had. In China, there were plenty of people to do the work. Mógū knew it was the Dynasty's belief that there was no need to import more mouths to feed.

They also had pirate ships that were protected by the Portuguese crown. These smaller boats were easily maneuverable and could get up fjords without difficulty. If those ships were captured, the ship itself was a treasure. Often, they contained expensive items that had already been pillaged; jewels, rare metals, opium and finely crafted swords, daggers and knives.

Mógū peered through the looking-glass and allowed her mind to wander a little.

In late November, as they sailed along the Pearl River Delta, Mógū spotted a few small ships that appeared to be coming from Macau.

Portuguese, she thought and remembered the altercation Po Tsai had with these same men in late summer. She made the signal to be prepared for a skirmish, although she didn't believe a few small Portuguese ships would try to take down their much larger fleet but she wouldn't be caught unprepared. She watched as the small junks around her answered her signal, adjusted their sails and prepared for possible gunfire or an all-out battle.

From the corner of her eye, she counted four more of the Portuguese ships coming from the opposite direction. Six against twenty-one, she still doubted they would engage in a fight. From her vantage point she could see the over-energetic captain, Miguel José de Arriaga Brum. His reputation proceeded him; she was well aware who he was and who he worked for. The hair on the back of her neck stood up as she wondered if the Qīng dynasty ships could be nearby. Captain Miguel José was close to the governor of Macau, perhaps even related. And the governor of Macau worked closely with the Chinese government. Her senses suggested this may be an ambush.

Cannon fire rang out from behind her, she ducked low to the deck and moved to another position pulling out her spy glass. Sure enough, the four ships coming from behind were firing on her fleet. She signaled for her large junk to turn into the large river mouth to continue up stream. More artillery fire from behind gave her an uneasy feeling.

In front of her were a dozen small junks facing off the two Portuguese ships and the eight junks behind her were already engaged in exchanging gunfire. As the large junk turned to move north, the smaller junks formed a semi-circle, covering and protecting her ship all while firing and being fired on. Although it became apparent the battle was inevitable, she still wasn't too worried. Their fleet had taken down bigger groups of ships. She was confident they had more men and more fire power.

Looking through the spy glass she was confused as to why two of the small junks were tilted towards each other. She watched closely and with horror realized they were sinking. She could see her men jumping to the water from the listing junks. Artillery fire was ramping up behind her too and she turned to see one of the junks on fire. She didn't need the spy glass to realize those men were also abandoning their ship and jumping into the cold water.

They had to get closer to these ships to board them and take them down. Her crews' strength was in hand to hand combat. She signaled for them to turn again, the sails adjusted and the huge junk began to turn when it took on artillery fire. One of the Portuguese ships had slipped past the two sinking junks and was nearing hers. Cannon fire rang out. A jolt rocked her ship, she was glad for the spikes in her boots that kept her upright. They were shooting back but their fire power was outnumbered. Everything about this encounter felt terribly wrong.

Chapter Twenty-Seven –Zhèng de Guǎfù Lives

The battle raged on for hours. When Mógū got a second to look up she made a mental note of how many junks were still visible. There was so much fire and smoke, it made it difficult for her to take an accurate inventory. They still had not been able to get close enough to their enemy to board and take them down. The Portuguese were fighting with everything they had from a few furlongs away. Burning projectiles were being cast at their vessels. It seemed there was no end to their fire power.

With horror she realized the big junk she was on had caught fire. The smoke billowed as the blaze tore through the vessel. It tilted to the side. Many of her men were jumping from the ship. She made the sign for surrender knowing there was no way the other junks could have seen it through the haze of the smoke. They had been engaged in this battle for nearly ten hours. It was clear they had lost.

Mógū jumped. Zhèng Yī flashed into her mind as she wondered at what point did he give up. Did he jump from his ship or did the Chinese kill him before the junk sunk? The cold water was a shock to her body. With urgency, she pushed her body towards the surface, the weight of her clothes hindering her progress.

Finally, she surfaced and took in a gulp of air assessing her surroundings. Several of the small junks were in various stages of being swallowed by the sea. Bodies floated near each wreckage, lifeless bodies bobbing in the waves. The huge junk listed severely. It would soon sink.

Men were yelling and the Portuguese were still firing. A cannon shot rang out. She needed to find something to hold on to or she would surely drown.

Crack! The noise rang out like thunder had split the sky. Mógū realized the sound was the heavy mast as it snapped free from the ship. With difficulty, she swam towards it. The waves and debris made it difficult for her to move through the water. She was able to hook her fingers into a crevasse on the large mass. Her heart was still racing but she felt momentarily safe from the depths of the sea.

The sun was setting. Through the smoke and light of dusk she saw five of the six Portuguese ships moving away from the fray. Of their twenty junks, none could be seen floating. Most were in ruin although she could not account for all of them. *What had gone wrong?* She realized with a great sense of guilt there were men clinging to the floating mast.

"Do you know if there is a junk capable of getting us home?" she asked one of the war-shocked men.

"Zhèng de Guǎfù?" he said, his eyes focusing on her face, "You're alive!" He turned in the water and shouted, "She's alive! Zhèng de Guǎfù lives!" Then he began to laugh and mutter, "She lives, the widow of Zhèng Yī lives."

Mógū heard a ripple of cheers as the news carried along the water, there were survivors, men she needed to get back to Lantau. "Is there a boat that can get us all back?" she hollered at him as she realized he was wrapped up in his own reflections and not capable of answering her. She scanned the horizon, dread rampant in her gut. She survived the battle but would drown before she could get home. It would be a quiet death, she thought, and again, Zhèng Yī's handsome face came to her mind. Did he drown? Would this be the gods' way of reuniting them? Zhèng Yī's face turned to Yīngshí's then Xióngshí's innocent features appeared, eventually her thoughts turned to Chūntáo and Po Tsai. No, today was not the day she would die, but the problem of getting back to shore loomed large.

Night had fallen and the water was black as ink. Debris floated around her, scattered every which way. Her teeth began to chatter as she listened to the noises around her. There were still some men yelling but they seemed far off. Then she heard the sound that would certainly save her life, splash, row, splash row, splash, row. At least one of the junks had survived. She tilted her head back and looked at the star-dappled sky.

"Thank you," she whispered to the heavens knowing Zhèng Yī was looking down at her, guiding the last junk towards her floating refuge. It seemed like hours when it was most likely only minutes before she saw the outline of the junk. Two men stood on the front holding the lanterns above their heads, one was in a red tinted case to aid in the navigation. It was on her right which she knew was the vessel's left. She yelled a battle cry and the other men holding on the mast echoed her shout. The junk coming towards them angled even closer.

Once the small junk was near them the rowing stopped. A rope ladder was cast down and Mógū and three other men started swimming towards their rescuer. Other men appeared from the blackness, splashing and cursing. In total fifteen of her crew had been clinging onto something floating, hoping to survive.

Throughout the night, they moved through the water retrieving survivors and the floating bodies of their dead. A rope sling had been fashioned to pull the deceased onto the small boat, the bodies piling up at the rear. Some faces Mógū recognized, other's she did not but she said a prayer to the ancestors for each as the corpses stacked up.

Chapter Twenty-Eight – You Can't Win Every Time

Light began to seep from the east giving them bearings. Mógū sat on the deck and watched the sun creep over the horizon.

"Zhèng de Guǎfù?" she heard over her shoulder and turned to see one of the crew. Most people had taken to calling her that, *Widow of Zhèng*, it honored her and disheartened her at the same time. "Thank the gods you live to see another sunrise," the man said as he handed her a cup of steaming tea. Gratefully she took it, the warmth seeping into her hands and through her bones. She breathed in the scent of the jasmine before she took a sip. The man was still talking, "...we'll be sure to send word you survived. Regardless of how many people we lost in this battle of the Tiger's Mouth, the Portuguese's main goal was to see you dead. I would give anything to see Governor's José's face when he learns of your survival."

"How many?" she asked and took another sip of the tea.

"Excuse me? How many what?"

"How many men did we lose?" She saw his mouth clamp shut, turning to a thin line, the creases of his face aging him ten years in ten seconds. "How many?" she demanded.

"We're not sure just yet," he replied sullenly.

Her eyes scanned behind the man where she saw two more junks following them home. "Our ships ride bow high loaded in the rear with the weight of our fallen warriors. What is your guess?"

"There are four junks still intact," he replied.

The fatigue turned to rage, she stood and screamed at him, "I could care less about the junks. How many lives did we lose?"

"Maybe two thousand," he said not meeting her eye, "maybe more."

The math started snapping in her head as her stomach clenched. They had left their port with twenty-one vessels and approximately four thousand men. Only half would be returning. The entire village would be clad in white for the next several months and there wouldn't be one person not affected by this massive loss.

"Po Tsai?" she heard the quake in her voice, the emotion barely contained.

"To my knowledge, Captain Cheung Po Tsai is alive and uninjured."

She nodded numbly. The sun began to warm the deck and her attention turned back to the recovered bodies. Guilt began to choke her and consciously she took a deep breath. Tears burned the back of her eyes as the lump in her throat made it difficult to breathe. What was she doing here? Was this really the way to live?

One loss, Zhèng Yǐ's voice in her head, *you can't win every time.* Tears fell from both eyes and a huge sob escaped from her lips. She curled into herself hiding her face as grief racked her entire body. *Ssshhh…* Zhèng Yǐ's comforting voice from beyond this life gave her little peace. She felt a hand on her shoulder and thought her longing for her husband was driving her into madness.

"Mógū?" It was Po Tsai. Her entire face snapped open to meet his concerned stare. "Are you alright?"

"No, yes," she gasped, "I'm…" Words failed her as the tears dried on her skin. She didn't want Po Tsai to see the raw emotion or anything that could be construed as weakness within her.

"I'm at a loss on how this happened," he said, the shock and confusion leaving him looking young and vulnerable.

"It's one loss," she heard Zhèng Yī's words come from her mouth, as if they were bottled inside of her, waiting to be released, "we can't win every time." She was hoping the words would offer Po Tsai a little comfort.

"A big loss," he said, as his face crumbled and sadness overtook his handsome face. She reached for him and he moved into her arms as he heaved a heavy sob into her shoulder. The enormity of great power began to form in her stomach and moved to her heart and head. It became obvious as Po Tsai wept in her arms, it would be her leading them to prosperity. It would be her seeking vengeance upon the Portuguese for this loss, she would be the one taking the Red Flag fleet into battle.

Returning was as difficult as she had imagined. The surviving men were fatigued and despondent. She and Po Tsai had begun to make two lists, one of the known survivors and one of the identifiable dead. There were clearly many bodies missing that would never be recovered. Those would be the hardest for the families left behind.

Mógū held back the emotion when she saw her sons. She wanted to give them the impression the battle had just been another day of work and routine but privately she wept. She wanted them to be educated and well-rounded so they may one day explore this world and not have to fight. She wanted them to be savvy businessmen, not pirates.

"You look like shit," Chūntáo told her as she rolled in a cart with a fresh pot of tea and two plates of food. She sat with Mógū, served her and then dished up a plate for herself. "Glad you survived," she said through a mouthful of food. Mógū nodded but didn't reply, she also had no appetite so the food sat in front of her untouched. She sipped the tea, the heat of it warming her from the inside out. "Are you done?" Chūntáo inquired.

Mógū looked at the untouched plate of food and shook her head confused. "I haven't even started, sister. I don't have much of an—"

"Oh, shut up, you ninny goat." Chūntáo rolled her eyes and took another bite of food. "I meant being a pirate, are you done with it? All this battling, men dead or dying, that, are you done with that?" she shook her head and turned her attention to the remaining food on her plate.

"No," Mógū said automatically, "not even close. I'll have my revenge. I'll not rest until the last drop of that bastard Miguel José's blood drips from my cutlass. I'll mount his head on—"

"Easy there, tiger," Chūntáo interjected, "a simple yes or no would have sufficed. Now eat and rest."

"I've got to see the families of those lost, tell them about the battle."

"It can wait until tomorrow, sister. There's not much daylight left and you need to rest. The news will be hard and heavy to deliver. You'll need all your strength."

Mógū knew her little sister was right. There wasn't much to do at that moment but enjoy the food and sleep. She would construct a plan for telling the villagers about the battle and the warriors they lost. It may be auspicious to have one week set aside to mourn all of the fallen together. Yes, that's what she would do, create one ceremony for the entire clan to mourn their dead. They could all collectively come together and honor those who had lost their lives. Traditional funerals were set over an entire week. It could be done.

As the plan formed in her head it became the most logical thing to do. The courtyard where she and Zhèng Yī were married would be big enough to gather everyone. Each family would have to break away to pray at their own family's altars, but after she spoke on behalf of the fleet, giving condolences once to a crowd instead of multiple times to each family became the most logical choice. She checked the moon chart and made note that the moon would be completely absent in 40 days. That would be the day for them all to come together and mourn. Tears would start to dry by that time and it would give her, Po Tsai and Chūntáo time to make the necessary arrangement for the white flowers, shrouds, and food for the seven days of the funeral.

Mógū's day to day life drained her spirit as her small entourage made their way through the villages to deliver the heavy news. It was as if she went through life in a haze, steeling herself from the grief and tears. Staying strong. The widows and fatherless children haunted her; their pained, pinched faces turning from shock to sorrow as she offered her condolences.

It was bittersweet when Yīngshí asked if could accompany her. On one hand he was able to connect with the children of the fallen men but on the other hand, she wanted to shield her son from this great sadness. In the end she realized it was his duty and honor to be part of such a substantial task. As the son of Zhèng Yī, everyone knew who he was, and Mógū observed him aging before her eyes. He would be a great leader some day; not a pirate, but an honest politician. Her mind flashed back to her flower boat days and she realized with sadness, the politicians were just as corrupt as her own fleet. Maybe Yīngshí could grow up to be a doctor instead, his bedside manner would be top-notch.

As they were finishing their difficult task in the last village she watched with pride as Yīngshí listened to an older boy's rant about the career choice of his dead father. When he was done, Yīngshí paused as if in thought and then with great respect told the young man, "Life is all about balance; there is no Yin without Yang. Your father was brave and worked hard to provide this life for you, for all of us. Not a scoundrel at all, he died a hero." Yīngshí bowed slightly and turned to join his mother. She was so proud she thought she would burst.

During the week of mourning, people shuffled from house to house offering their well-wishes. The white flowers laid at each home's entrance signified which families had suffered loss. It seemed to Mógū there were white flowers at every door she passed.

The great feast night was successful. Tables of food and drink had been laid out for the living and the dead. Family urns filled with fresh goat's blood were added to the table to honor the deceased. After the meal Po Tsai and Chūntáo urged Mógū to speak, to say something to the people who had suffered a similar loss as hers.

She used Yīngshí's Yin and Yang example to address the crowd. What they did was lawless, yes, but what the Qīng dynasty and Portuguese monarchy was doing was no better. She mentioned the British Queen's skull and crossbones fleet even though she had never actually encountered one. The bottom line was, the men who had died did so for their families. They died so their families may live a better life, one without the pangs of hunger, or want. They were indeed heroes even though the governments of surrounding territories would disagree. She could hear the crowd's murmur of approval and it spurred her on to the topic of her late husband. It seemed everyone's common denominator when it came to their grief was their loyalty to Zhèng Yī.

"I'm sure Zhèng Yī is as great a leader in Naraka as he was here on earth. Together they will navigate the mazes of Diyú and be reborn into a higher world where we will all meet them again one day," she finished her speech and gazed into the teary eyes of those listening.

Chapter Thirty – 1809

She could see two large cargo boats with several dozen smaller boats sailing around them like a dark, billowing cloak. At first, she thought the flags were the black elusive skull and crossbones flags, but after watching for several minutes she made out the primary colored crown in the center of the white field, the ships of Maria the Mad of Portugal. Dona Maria had her young son, João, in training for the monarchy. Mógū had heard political rumors that Brazil and Algarve were in Maria's scope to increase their kingdom and wealth.

Today, however; Mógū would be taking a piece of that prosperity. She counted sixty-eight of the small boats. She was confident the two big ones were full of African slaves. Her fleet was now over eight hundred with close to ten thousand men fighting with her; she doubted she would even leave her ship for this skirmish.

She watched the small ships in front of hers begin to circle and encourage the crew on the opposing boats to surrender. Often that worked, especially when the sailors knew they were outnumbered and certainly were gambling with their lives. The Portuguese were not that navy though, they would fight. As she watched her ships approach, she could see by the stance of the men on board, they knew it too and were preparing for combat.

Snaps of sails being brought down around her made her realize her junk was not going in to fight. She would only watch this brawl, she realized with a touch of disappointment. The boats closest to her were already under attack. Her men had flung large hooks attached to thick ropes on both sides of the small boat. She could hear the *bap, bap* of guns being fired create a rhythm, then farther away a larger *pow* she knew was a cannon.

The Portuguese ship she was watching was already secured by her men, they were pulling it closer to them so they could board it and overthrow the captain. It swayed between the two junks and Mógū thought about a fly trapped in a spider web, the movements futile, the outcome prearranged.

Pow! Bap! Her attention was diverted to the others around her as each boat's battle began.

Once they returned from overtaking the small Portuguese fleet, Mógū's suspicions were confirmed; the two bigger boats were full of slaves. The hundreds of dark-skinned humans were spread out along the shore, some had formed little groups, others were moving through the throngs as if looking for someone. All of these stolen souls made the minor victory bittersweet. Chūntáo lumbered up to Mógū carrying a vat of steamed rice.

"Wu Jun made this and there's broth too," Mógū looked at the offering and realized the prisoners must be famished.

"That's not near enough," she commented.

"Of course, it's not, ninny, I'm only one person. How do you expect me to carry enough rice for all these people? There's more, we have plenty in the food storage. Wu Jun is making it."

Mógū nodded knowing Chūntáo was right. There were piles of burlap bagged rice. Chūntáo made a make-shift table and set down the vat of rice. She returned to the cart and brought out a cask of the broth with a wooden ladle.

"What we don't have is a way to serve everyone," she said as she set the broth near the rice and went back to the cart for another vat of rice. Mógū's mind flashed to the cave where all the treasures were stored, she remembered several fancy porcelain dish sets that has been acquired. She smiled to herself thinking of the Africans on the beach eating their rice off of British flatware.

"Let's make it into balls," she said as she scooped a handful of rice and rolled it between her hands to make a single serving.

"Great idea," Chūntáo agreed and copied Mógū's rice ball. "They can sip the broth from the ladle. Maybe we should have them get in a line." She shrugged at Mógū who nodded her agreement.

Mógū moved towards the beach trying to decide how to communicate to the foreigners they needed to line up to receive a rice portion when she heard a muffled scream. Her eyes darted towards the sound and she realized one of her men was accosting one of the black women from behind. The woman struggled to get free as the man rammed himself into her from behind while holding his hand over her mouth. Many onlookers gaped at the scene not knowing what to do. The black men, if not half starved to death, would have certainly had the strength to stop the rape.

"Hey," Mógū screamed, "that behavior is reserved for a marriage bed."

"Marriage bed," he guffawed but he didn't stop or even slow down as Mógū approached.

"Is this your new wife?" she bellowed and took a scarf from her waist and wrapped it around the man's arm. "You are going to marry this girl." He turned his attention to her as a look of confusion washed over his face, she attached the other end of the scarf to the frightened woman. "Lovemaking is for marriage, this woman is now your wife, she will be the only woman you'll poke your penis into, do you understand me?" Mógū could feel the rage boil from her guts. The black woman was clawing at the scarf on her wrist trying to get it off as the perplexed man took in the most recent development. He jerked his arm so the woman stumbled and reached out to Mógū so she wouldn't fall. The woman's eyes were wild with fear.

"Fuck you," the man said and spat at Mógū. She quickly stepped aside still holding the woman up. With his free hand he adjusted his clothing to cover his genitals then moved his attention the knotted fabric around his wrist.

"If you cheat with another woman, the punishment is death. You've picked your bride with the small brain in your jíjí." Mógū snapped. Her words came out hot and fast. She was livid this man would misrepresent her people by accosting a guest. These people were not her slaves, nor would they be, ever.

"Maybe I didn't speak loud enough," the man said, "fuck you, I don't take orders from a woman."

Rage roiled from Mógū. Like a snake striking, fast and without mercy, she pulled out her cutlass. One fluid swipe through the man's neck shut him up. His head landed at the feet of the woman he had just raped. She began to scream, high pitched and horrified. The body of her rapist made a little jerk and then fell, pulling the terrified woman to the ground. Her screams escalated into full terror as she kicked and twisted attempting to free herself. Mógū's sharp, bloody blade quickly came down and cut the scarf still binding the woman to the dead man. Once free she scampered away sobbing.

Mógū realized all eyes were on her, their crew, Chūntáo and all the blacks. Silence rippled through the crowd. Mógū raised the bloody cutlass above her head, "Anyone else have a problem taking orders from a woman?" she shouted into the stillness. There were no replies, she turned deliberately towards her audience. "Unless you've picked a partner to enter into matrimonial nuptials with there will be no sex or your fate will be as sure as this piece of dung," she indicated the decapitated corpse at her feet. "No sex!" she screamed and then repeated the order to drive her point home, "No sex!"

Tears burned the backs of her eyes as Zhèng Yī came into her mind. She missed him. How would he have handled the situation? She hoped her actions would have made him proud. With trepidation, everyone returned to their tasks giving the dead man a wide berth.

Chapter Thirty-One – Code of Law

"Don't think I didn't see what you did out there today," Po Tsai said to Mógū as they sat for their evening meal, "No sex, huh?"

"It's a distraction," she commented without looking at him. He shrugged and nodded then took another bite of food. "I'll kill a rapist any day."

"What about consensual sex?" Po Tsai asked.

"I'll behead the man and drown the woman," she snapped back, "I'll tie cannonballs to her ankles to ensure she ends up at the bottom of the sea."

"That makes perfect sense," Po Tsai commented.

"Thieves. Dead," her jaw was set tight.

"Reasonable," Po Tsai commented and turned his attention back to his food.

Yes, these were the rules now on her ship. *Obey or perish*. She could feel the blood rush through her veins remembering the afternoon. The woman's look of terror, her screams, the noise the man's head made when it hit the dirt. She would have to uphold the new rules, she would not have anyone serving under her be terrified or accosted like that woman. No, not while she was in charge.

Dinner had been served late that night as they had so much to attend to providing for the two hundred and twenty kidnapped Africans. Most of them had created their own camp near the water. Mógū posted men at the trailhead that went down to the water to give them, and herself, a small feeling of security.

"I think we should take them back to their native land," Po Tsai said through bites of his dumpling.

Mógū absently nodded her head, her mind still spinning from the new code of laws she would implement on her junk. *If there are deserters, I will hunt them down and cut off their ears.*

"If I go now, I could return by summer," Po Tsai was still talking and she noticed he was being too nonchalant in this conversation. She realized he had already been planning taking the Africans back.

"We could always cut a space for them and they could create their own—"

"Their own village?" he snapped.

"Sure, why not?" her mind was still reeling over the new rules she would implement, *those committing adultery, beheaded,* but this conversation was important and she needed Po Tsai's input on what to do.

"They don't belong here," he said.

"Maybe not, but they could be comfortable," she replied.

"If you were kidnapped and taken to a new land against your will, would you want to start anew or go back?"

He had a point and she nodded. "Do you want the boys and me to accompany you on this voyage?"

Po Tsai shook his head. "No. Who would continue to run our little empire? Chūntáo?" Mógū couldn't help it, she grinned at Po Tsai picturing her little sister as captain of the large junk. "You are much more valuable here in the bigger picture of things."

She couldn't help but agree. With her new Code of Law, she would be more respected by her crew, and feared. Her confidence grew, she could navigate and command without Po Tsai. In fact, a few months without him may be pleasant.

"When are you leaving?" She smiled and finished her dinner.

In a matter of days, three of the four largest junks had been stocked with enough food, water and rice wine for six months, the maximum time the expedition should be gone. Most of the Africans were anxious. They had rested on the beaches, their strength returned. The black men that had joined their armada spoke a different language than the blacks from this particular ship. Mógū learned most of the African villages had their own language or even a different dialect of the same. They had been able to convey their intentions through rudimentary hand signals and a drawing in the sand. She knew returning them to their homeland was merely an excuse for Po Tsai to sail to Cape Town. It was the decent thing to do. She wasn't going to kill people just to kill. She wasn't a monster. But she would demand the respect and loyalty from her crew. She wouldn't hesitate to end someone's life to attain that authority.

Most nights, Mógū had observed the Africans' routines from a ledge with a nice vantage point overlooking the bay. It's where she had sat for days while she waited for Zhèng Yī's ship to appear. Their singing brought a smile to her face, it was so unique, like nothing she had ever heard.

A noise caused a moment of angst before she recognized the sound of Po Tsai's footsteps approaching. He appeared from the darkness and gracefully lowered himself to the ground to sit next to her. She acknowledged him without speaking, her attention to the encampments below. After a few moments he said, "Sitting up here makes me miss Zhèng Yī."

"Me too," she agreed. She raised her face to the quarter moon.

"We shall be husband and wife when I return?" there was more of a question in his voice than she expected. She realized it had all been decided for him and they hadn't actually discussed it since the day with Zhèng Sì many weeks before. That morning seemed like an eternity ago.

"It makes the most sense," she said and turned to look at him, "since it seems I must be married to command a ship, I need a husband."

He was already staring at her. She had been seeing a more vulnerable side of him since the morning after the battle when he had wept in her arms.

"I could trust no other, Po Tsai," she said gently.

"Do you think Zhèng Yī would approve?" he asked.

"Yes, I think Zhèng Yī would have approved," she agreed, the words ringing true between them.

"I dreamed of it," he answered turning his attention to the moon, "in my dream, Zhèng Yī came to me. He was excited about a treasure." Momentarily, Mógū felt a pang of longing for Zhèng Yī to visit her dreams. "He told me I must protect this treasure with my life, I couldn't imagine what could have been so important until I looked down. You were lying prone, eyes closed and your lips blue. I thought you were dead but when I reached for you your eyes opened and gave me such a fright, I woke."

Mógū felt a twist of a grin. The dream was favorable and she thought it would be just the type of prank Zhèng Yī would pull, offering her to Po Tsai but letting him think she was dead. She felt the warmth of his hand taking hers. He was putting something solid into her palm. A cloud passed over the moon causing the light to dim considerably. Even without it, she knew he had given her a ring.

"Where did you get this?" she asked.

"From one of those black women down there." He motioned to the camps below. "I cut the finger off of the woman wearing it. I still have it if you'd like to make a necklace with it."

"Po Tsai, you didn't!" she gasped horrified. She tried to hand the ring back to him but he wouldn't take it.

"You're right, I didn't," he said after a chuckle, "it was my mother's."

"You have a mother?" she joked, taking in the ring now the cloud had passed, and the moon's reflective light reappeared. It was lovely, the deep red stone seemed black with the limited light.

"I stole this ring when I ran away," his tone took on a faraway quality, as if the story itself was taking him back to his youth. "My intention was to sell it and buy a ticket on a ship going anywhere out of

Sheng Jing." Mógū turned and regarded him. She could see the boy he had once been in his shadowed features.

"So, what happened?"

"I met Zhèng Yī." The love that panged in his voice made her own heart ache. "He took the ring from me in exchange for passage on his junk. For many years he had it. I assumed it was sold or traded but then, on my twenty-second birthday, he gave it back to me. It was all I had left to remember my family and life before I fled."

"Why did you flee?"

"I was young. I wanted adventure, I wanted to travel. My parents were already negotiating a marriage between me and my second cousin. She was pretty enough but I was attracted to men too. I couldn't imagine myself settling into a routine labeled husband, working for my father and his brothers and that was it. Life over," he said shaking his head, his jaw muscles set looking every bit his age now, "it seemed like a trap. So, one day I took the ring from my mother's small box of special trinkets. Once everyone had settled in for the night, I slipped out of my family's *fángzi*. I went to the docks and slept under the stars with the sea's waves whispering to me. I met Zhèng Yī the very next day and my life started anew by his side." A long moment of silence passed between them.

"I loved him so much," she said quietly.

"Me too," he agreed.

She slipped the ring on her first finger, the only one it fit. She leaned over and laid her head on his shoulder, his arm reflexively wrapped around her.

My life started anew by his side, Po Tsai's words echoed in her head.

Chapter Thirty-Two – Farewell and Be Well

The sun woke Mógū the next morning. Her thoughts flashed to the quiet walk back from the cliffs to the house with Po Tsai. She touched the new ring on her first finger then the emerald one on her third. A red stone and a green one, as opposite as the men themselves. Her marriage to Po Tsai would be one of convenience and business without the passion and love she had before. There was loyalty and mutual admiration. It would be enough.

Within a week, the big boats were loaded and ready to depart for their half year journey to Africa and back. Goodbyes were clipped and felt businesslike.

"Take care of your mother and Chūntáo," Po Tsai had said to Yīngshí. The young man bowed respectfully as his younger brother answered verbally.

"I'm a warrior too, Po Tsai. May I help?" Everyone smiled at him and it eased some of the tension that seemed to be laced through the air.

"Of course, you can," Po Tsai answered, a smile flashing through his eyes even though it didn't reach his mouth.

"Farewell and be well," Mógū said to Po Tsai. He nodded and turned to leave.

"Bye bye," the children called as he boarded the giant junk, "bye bye."

The big junks began to pull from the docks and Mógū felt a longing to go too. Her heart yanked and seemed to speed up, her gut tightening. The yearning was not necessarily for Po Tsai, but for the adventure itself. Chūntáo's voice interrupted her reverie.

"That's a relief and a half."

"What is?" Mógū asked. The boys had broken free from her and were running down the dock back to the shore.

"All those mouths to feed, it's a relief we're not cooking for all those people every day."

"You cook?" Mógū jested.

"No but it's exhausting to watch Měiyīng and Wu Jun work so hard." Chūntáo giggled. "I'm joking but it's true. We now know what our limits are for overnight guests, that is for sure."

They walked back to the big house with the children scampering in front of them playing deep in an imaginary world. Mógū's mind floated back to her own childhood. Had she ever been as carefree as Yīngshí and Xióngshí?

A brief glimpse of her father flashed through her mind. She was running towards his fishing boat, he was knelt down to her level, his arms flung as wide as his smile. When she had reached him, he scooped her up and tossed her into the air. She saw her shadow below disconnect from his hands and then fall safely back. He nuzzled his scruffy face into her neck and set her back down on the ground. Her mother had then caught up to them and the energy of the moment changed to business, fish, food, money.

It didn't take long for Mógū's routine to be business as usual. Their food supply had taken a big hit with the extra two hundred souls they had been feeding the last month.

The protection tax collection was the main source of income at this time and she didn't feel it necessary to raid for more loot. The Battle at Tiger's Mouth was too fresh in her head, so many men they had recently lost. Plus, with Po Tsai and his men gone, looting seemed too risky.

To still make a bit of a presence as they traveled, Mógū got in the habit of taking the last large junk with twenty smaller junks up and down the coast. It was a show for the poor villages yet enough of a force they could hold their own if they were to stumble upon Qīng or the skull and crossbones pirates. She'd even be ready if the Portuguese were to return.

Often, she didn't embark at the smaller ports unless it was a stop where she wanted to shop, and since the massive funeral, she hadn't felt like acquiring anything new, not even for her sons. A delivery system had been worked out for trading and communicating up and down the shores of Dai Nam. At each port, letters and small packages were picked up and dropped off. At every stop there was a designated runner who met their ship and took the deliverable items. Mógū had started a new ledger for it and required the runners to make their marks on the pages when they dropped off or picked up items to be shipped.

She began thinking there could be a small charge for these deliveries. The tax collections were already on somewhat of a schedule. These other items could be shipped on the same schedule creating another stream of income. Correspondence throughout the coast could be consistent. In fact, with some help, it could be continued to other countries like Macau and mainland China. Communication of all kinds was distributed regularly for royalty and government; her system could be for all people of these little villages. She was going port to port anyway, why not increase the money she collected and provide a service to the people like nothing they had ever experienced.

Chapter Thirty-Three – Return of Captain Miguel José

Three months passed and the village began to heal from losing so many husbands and fathers. It felt different, now the women and children were all fending for themselves. Mógū seemed to take on a bit of responsibility for them. She instructed Chūntáo to travel around the village each week and distribute rice and salt to those families in need. Yīngshí had taken up as Chūntáo's helper. Mógū felt pride each time she saw a glimpse of the man he would eventually become. He was compassionate and serious yet had a great head for business even at such a young age.

On the next tax collection run she would need to get a few dozen sacks of rice and at least a hundred of the fibrous leaves to roll the rice into. It was time consuming for the kitchen staff to roll the rice into the leaves but it made distribution easier and the rice stayed fresher by preserving in this way.

She would also check with the local fishermen to ensure they were bringing in enough fish to feed the village. She would ask Chūntáo to see if there were any mothers who may need extra rations. If so, she would personally buy the fish from the locals to help the widowed mothers.

As they made their way north on the next tax collection run, Mógū implemented the new correspondence charge. There were a few people who didn't want to pay and their letters weren't accepted but most wanted their communication to be delivered, and if they didn't have money, they offered an egg or, in some cases, a chicken. It made the most sense to use these offerings to subsidize the food for the poorest of her villagers. She turned the ledger over and upside down and opened the binding. She would keep track of the trade offerings on this side of the ledger and the correspondence and parcels on the other. She would make money, there would be extra food for the widows, and the correspondence would continue to be delivered on a systematic schedule.

As they headed back to Lantau on the last tax collection run before the lunar new year, Mógū felt enthusiastic about the changes happening in her life. The year of the Goat was beginning with the next new moon. Peace and kindness, justice and strength would be the allures of the up and coming year.

Mógū was engrossed in her new plan with the delivery system as she made notes in the ledger. She studied the map that was laid out on the big table. From Seoul, Korea all the way south to Malaysia, she knew there were boats traveling weekly, perhaps daily. There had to be records at each port as to what ships came in regularly. It would be possible to have a designated spot for patrons to drop off and retrieve their correspondence. Perhaps the charges could be based on the weight of the item being shipped.

A knock on the door snapped her from being lost in thought to the present moment. It opened before she could respond. A lackey stepped in; she saw worry on his face.

"Madam Zhèng, I, um, the quartermaster said to—" he stammered on his words.

"What?" she was irritated at the disruption and more so at this boy who couldn't get his words straight.

"Ships," he managed to spit out, "about a dozen, maybe Portuguese."

"What? Where?" she was on her feet and moving past the messenger not listening to his stuttered reply.

Once on deck she looked through the spy glass. She recognized the Portuguese flag immediately. As she counted, she realized there were three times as many ships as the boy had said, at least thirty, perhaps more. The hair stood up on the back of her neck when she identified the lead ship in the fleet.

"Captain Miguel José," she murmured.

"Who?" the quartermaster asked.

"Miguel José de Arriaga Brum," she spat each syllable as if it tasted nasty in her mouth, "the captain from Tiger's Mouth." She heard an audible intake of breath as the man realized who they were preparing to confront. Rage and revenge twisted Mógū's stomach into a knot. The faces of the widows and fatherless children paraded in her mind. "Today, we shall serve justice for our villages' loss."

"How?" the young quartermaster asked. Most of the men were green, inexperienced, many had taken the places of their fallen fathers.

"With the blood of our enemies," she answered snapping the spyglass back into the smallest size.

"Yeah, but how?" he asked, his voice sounding small and unsure, "there's way more of them than us."

"We'll work together and take them down one at a time like they did to us at Tiger's mouth," she was moving now and making arm signals to the smaller ships. They responded by maneuvering closer to the big junk forming a tight circle around her ship. As she moved, she shouted to the crew asking questions about the amount of ammunition and number of men on board each boat. They had twenty-one vessels and Miguel's men had at least three dozen. They weren't that outnumbered; they had battled before with smaller numbers than their opponents. This battle was too important to lose.

By nightfall, she would be victorious or dead.

Chapter Thirty-Four – Zhèng Yī Would be Proud

Mógū ordered the men to bring the cannons to the front of the large junk. She calculated the angle of cannonball knowing it would shoot over the smaller junks when the Portuguese got close. She also instructed a few of the men to load every rifle they had on board and lay them in a row near the bow of the big junk.

"We need at least one man to reload as fast as our men can fire," she explained. They nodded in understanding as the junks' formation began to move as one towards Miguel's spread-out fleet. Reopening the spyglass, she searched for Miguel's boat. When she found it, she realized he was looking at her through his own spyglass. She wasn't sure if he saw her or felt her hard stare but he lowered his spyglass from his eye and smiled wide, then to her surprise, bowed low and lurid. He was mocking her! That act enraged her as much as the deaths of two thousand of her men. It was as if he were pouring kerosene on a flame. Her jaw locked in rage and she felt the anger taking hold. She would avenge her village.

For a moment she wished Po Tsai was with her, then she longed for Zhèng Yī. It dawned on her this was her battle, neither of the men in her life were here to witness how the battle would play out. Triumphant or not, everything in this fight was hers to own.

Three of the Portuguese ships advanced. They were spread out as if to encircle her fleet. It was the most logical and predictable maneuver. She signaled for them to turn portside. A move that would not have been anticipated. It was the furthest ship from the rest of the fleet and she knew it would be the easiest to take down. They would have to hurry before the other ships came to its defense.

The Portuguese boat moved further away from the other two just as Mógū had expected. It would be foolhardy to attack one on twenty-one. The two other ships had adjusted their sails and were beginning to move towards their prey. Three more ships came from Miguel's fleet headed towards them. The first shots rang out from the Portuguese ship as they bared down on it. She didn't want them to fire back just yet, they were limited on their ammunition and wanted to make every shot count. She held her fists above her head, the signal to hold off on any gunfire. More shots were fired towards them and she hoped her men were crouched down and protected to miss the buckshot.

After a few more moments of gunfire she heard the smaller junk in front of hers bump into the Portuguese boat. It was then she gave the signal to attack. She turned her attention to the other ships approaching and listened as her men swarmed the boat taking the lives of the Portuguese men onboard.

The next boat was getting very close and she shouted for the cannon to be angled towards the oncoming ship. Mógū rushed to the railing and looked over, one of her small junks was exactly where it was supposed to be, nearly butted up to her own ship. She motioned for the cannon to be tilted upwards slightly. She could see the confused expressions on the men's faces but they did as they were ordered, no questions asked.

Once she felt the angle of cannon was right, she made the signal for it to be fired. As she suspected, the ball curved up slightly before descending. It landed on the bow of the Portuguese ship with a loud crack. She knew she had hit the mark, the boat immediately started to list forward as the men on board scrambled to get a few shots off before their boat sank. She made a motion to send a second cannon ball into the deck and it hit its mark again, this time taking off the figurehead and gouging a large hole in the boat's bow.

She turned her attention to the first boat; her men had secured it. She could see bloody bodies on the deck and many men flailed in the water. Her men were gathering the Portuguese arms and bringing them to their own junk. One of the men made an all clear signal. She gave an order to set fire to the ship and within minutes flames were leaping up the masts and engulfing the now sinking ship.

Two down, she thought as she turned her attention back to the sinking boat with the cannonball holes in the deck. A few of the Portuguese men fired rifles as they passed, moving towards their third ship. She held the spyglass to her eye to see where Captain Miguel José's ship had gone. As she suspected his ship had fallen back behind the others, *coward*.

The large junk sat so high in the water she had a bird's eye view of all the smaller skirmishes below. One by one they conquered each of the Portuguese ships that approached. Her decision to keep all the junks close around her paid off as they were a much greater force clustered together. The advantageous angle of the cannon also proved to be perfect as they were able to do indefensible damage from above.

Mógū dashed from port to starboard shouting orders and assessing the damage to their fleet. They had lost two junks so far. Some of the surviving men were able to reach the huge junk and board it. There was a makeshift infirmary on the third deck and she was grateful to have such a humongous junk for this particular battle. Even though their ships were outnumbered, their men were not. Fearless if not heartbroken warriors made up her fleet. She knew, like herself, they were all seeking retaliation for some loss they had encountered from the battle of Tiger's Mouth.

Mógū continued command from the upper deck of the huge junk until there were only a few ships left. The number of her men boarding them had increased by ten-old and she felt confident that there wouldn't be any reason for them to take those ships without destroying them. This battle was hers; victorious against Miguel José. *Zhèng Yī would be proud*, and as an afterthought, *Po Tsai too*.

She watched as the hand to hand combat commenced on the remaining ships. Miguel's was so close she could see him wielding his sword, her men were holding their own.

Remembering the way Zhèng Yī swung onto the lead ship of those they took down gave her an idea. She took a crossbow and attached a sturdy rope to the quarrel and the other end to the railing of the huge junk. She fired it down at Miquel's boat. She tightened the railing rope and took her leather sash off. She looped it around the rope and took in a deep breath.

She jumped before she could overthink and change her mind. The leather held her as she slid down the rope. Looking down caused her stomach to fall into the crevice between the two hulls and her breath to get caught in her lungs. She was moving much faster than she had expected and when she was close to the deck of Miquel's ship, she let go with one hand so the leather would fall away.

Adrenaline coursed through her as she landed. Her knees bent hard and she felt the spikes of her shoes dig deep into the wood. She rocked forward and realized they were stuck. Looking up, her eyes met José's. The sounds of swords striking against each other surrounded her, the strong smell of blood left a metallic whiff in her nose. Her sense of survival became overwhelming. A flash of the old nun's cat impression flashed in her mind. Mógū pulled her cutlass as she growled low, her face in an animal-like grimace.

Miguel Jose's face flashed confusion for a moment as one of Mógū's men looped a leather wrap around his neck. Miguel gasped and writhed as he swung his sword behind him. Her warrior was strong and smart and kept out of harm's way. She ceased the moment of confusion and shifted all of her weight forward releasing the shoes. With agility and force she shot forward and brought her cutlass to Miguel's throat.

"I want to kill you, you must know that," her words came out hot and clipped. Miquel glared at her. He was no threat, her men had him completely restrained. The clamor of the combat around her had stilled.

She knew the majority of the men standing were the Red Flag Fleet. She glanced around and saw there was at least one man with the Portuguese uniform. He was also being held by one of her men. She saw the whites of his eyes flash in fear. Her attention turned back to the captain. "Death would be the easy way out, no, I'm not going to end your life." Mummers of confusion could be heard rippling through the men. "Go back to your crazy bitch queen and tell her even though you outnumbered us three to one a poor girl from Guǎngzhōu emerged victorious. This is the Red Flag Fleet's territory, my territory. Understand? If she wants to continue this fruitless assault against me and my men, I'll track her down myself and drive my cutlass clean through her pious soul. Got it?" Mógū picked up Miguel's sword from the deck at his feet, "I think I'll keep this as a token of our foray today," she cooed to him, "something to remember you by." She turned and looked at the men that surrounded her. There were three men with the Portugal colors on. "How many men do you need to sail this ship, Miguel José de Arriaga Brum?" she sneered at him.

"I could sail it myself," he spat.

Using his sword, she beheaded one of the men then stabbed another leaving only one standing.

"Did you hear my message for Mad Maria?" she asked the remaining Portuguese man. He nodded, his face was frozen in an expression of horror. "Good. See to it she gets my message, I don't trust your captain."

Chapter Thirty-Five – Year of the Goat

The new year would ring in on the new moon kicking off the fifteen-day celebration. Mógū was in Zhèng Yī's room preparing an offering to him on the little table they had used to smoke opium so often. She included an orange and a pomegranate, several coins and an ornate tobacco pipe loaded with fresh ground leaves. Her heart was heavy as she thought about her lost husband.

"You'd be so proud of your sons," she said more to herself, "they are growing into fine young men. Watch over Po Tsai for us and deliver him back safely, husband, please and thank you."

Chūntáo bounced into the room. "Hey sister, don't be a glum ninny, it's a new year, a fresh start. The year of the Goat! Bbbaaaaa. Get it? Ninny goat?"

Mógū took a deep breath and couldn't help but smile. "Bbbaaa."

"Hello Zhèng Yī," Chūntáo said and placed her hand respectfully on the orange, "wish you were here." She took a lit incense and touched it to a new one, causing it to start to smolder, a sign of reverence and goodwill. The words and actions caused tears to spring into Mógū's eyes. Chūntáo threw her arms around her and whispered into her ear, "Let's get drunk." Mógū nodded and pulled away while getting control of her emotions.

"How are the plans for this week's festivities?"

"Oh, everything is all set," Chūntáo's arm was still around Mógū and she steered her from the dead man's room and down the corridor as she talked. "Wu Jun and Měiyīng have the menu prepped and the decorations are being brought up from the storage house. I'm letting Xióngshí have Yīngshí's red party wear and I'm almost done with a new outfit for him. He's gotten so tall since last year."

Mógū nodded. "The fireworks?"

"Also, ready when you are," she answered.

"Do we know who's coming?"

"Zhèng Sì's family for sure, and Měiyīng's husband and children. We haven't heard from San's yet but I'm guessing they will make an appearance too. I mean where else would they ring in the new year but here?"

They had reached the large kitchen where the boys were helping Wu Jun and Měiyīng with the nightly meal preparation.

"I don't want Yīngshí's old clothes," Xióngshí whined, "I want new party pants too. Why does Yīngshí always get new clothes and I always get his old ones?"

"It comes with being the little brother," Mógū answered and put her arms around her youngest son.

"Are you young men ready to scare off Nián this year?" Chūntáo asked.

"Who's Nain?" Xióngshí asked, his attention diverted.

"It's the monster that comes to eat bad children," Yīngshí said dramatically, "that's why you have to be good and wear red or Nián will eat you."

"Mommy, is that true?" his round face had drained of color as his eyes searched hers.

"It is," Chūntáo piped in, "we have extra loud and bright fireworks this year. Nián is very afraid of those. Don't you worry Xióngshí, we won't let that beast eat you." She reached out and tickled him in his ribs causing him to squirm tighter against Mógū's chest. She relished in his affection and was grateful he was still small enough to fit on her lap.

"Will Po Tsai be back by then?" Yīngshí asked.

"No dear," Mógū said, "but we'll have another festival when he returns."

"Bonus!" Chūntáo hollered, "Two celebrations this year, you lucky lads."

A loud knock on the front door caused them all to leave the kitchen duties to Měiyīng and Wu Jun. Mógū opened the door to see three horse-drawn carts full of red decorations. The large dragon head could be seen on the top. This was Mógū's favorite part of the New Year celebration. Their dragon was made of cloth stretched over a bamboo frame. It had thirteen joints and was considered very auspicious. The Dragon Dance was imperative to ensure the new year was full of wisdom, power and wealth. The spirit of the celebration was beginning to creep into Mógū's heart. A new year, a new beginning.

"Oh, I almost forgot," the delivery man said and pulled a white envelope from a pocket and handed it to Mógū.

"What's this?" she asked as she looked at the wax seal. White envelopes were never good news. They almost always announced sickness or death.

"It's from Maria the Mad," the man replied.

"Oh my, what does it say?" Chūntáo was suddenly curious.

"Miguel José is dead," the delivery man said.

"What? When? How?" Mógū glanced at her sons who were gratefully more interested in the carts full of New Year's decorations than the dull conversation the adults were having. The news came as a shock as she knew he was very much alive only a month before when she had spared his life. She broke the wax seal. There were two sheets of parchment. She scanned the Portuguese words that were neatly written in calligraphy on the top one. "I don't understand."

"It's a death certificate. I'm not sure why it was sent to you, but according to what I heard when the letter was entrusted to me, he killed himself."

Mógū's brow furrowed. "No, that can't be right."

"The report I got from the letter carrier, was when Miguel's ship could see the landscape of his motherland, he put a pistol under his chin and fired."

"Why would he do that?" Chūntáo asked. The boys were now paying attention to their conversation.

"According to the only other survivor, he was too ashamed to tell his queen he got his ass kicked by a woman."

It wasn't the end of Miguel's life she had pictured, but it was surprisingly satisfying. What great news to share with Po Tsai when he returned. A contented grin spread across Mógū's mouth as she looked at the second page from the envelope. It appeared to be a bulletin with a bounty on her life. Five hundred escudos was all the text she recognized. A crude sketch of her likeness stared up at her. She was lost in thought as the delivery man prepared to leave.

"Only five hundred?" Chūntáo announced reading over her shoulder, "Mógū's head is worth ten times that."

"Do you know if she got my message?" Mógū asked the delivery man.

"Cleary," he answered as he mounted his horse and left leaving the carts full of the holiday decorations.

Chapter Thirty-Six – New Year 1810

The year of the Goat celebration was indeed glorious Everyone came together to heal and hope for the best for the new year. Everything from the food to the fireworks came off without a hitch. The boys were thrilled with their red envelopes full of coins for the best wishes for the new year. The dragon dance and parade through the village square was cheerful and lively. Mógū and Chūntáo celebrated each day between the new moon and full.

"This is my favorite time of year," Chūntáo had slurred one evening as they watched a small fireworks display.

"Of course, it is, it's everyone's favorite time of year," Mógū answered not taking her eyes off the dancing flames of the stationary bangers.

"It's not though, some people don't like new years, they like old years."

"You're drunk." Mógū chuckled and turned her attention to Chūntáo.

"I am, yes," Chūntáo agreed, "but I'm right." Their eyes met and they both burst into fits of laughter.

"I'm ready for a clean slate."

Chūntáo nodded and threw her arms around her best friend. "I know honey, I know."

On the last day of the New Year celebration, Mógū took a food offering to the family shrine just as the sun crested the horizon. She knew the preparations were being made for them to leave again and head to Ha Long Bay. The full moon was only days away, soon it would be time to go back to work. There would only be two or three more moons before Po Tsai would return and their life together would begin for better or worse. And then what?

She loved the sea but yearned to explore, instead of a routine run up the coast of Dai Nam and back. She thought of Po Tsai and the adventures he must have experienced over the last few months. Did the black people make it back to their motherland? There were so many of them, there could have been a mutiny on board. They could have overthrown Po Tsai and his crew; she may never see him again. The thought crashed down on her with a wave of depression.

Mógū had been so buoyant during the new year celebrations, excited for her life but now she missed Zhèng Yī. She wanted to be a full-time mother and explore the world with her sons at her sides. She even missed Po Tsai. No longer did she want to collect taxes, nor did she want any sort of routine. She knelt in front of Zhèng Yī's memorial and pulled from her pack the opium pipe, candle and flint. She lit the candle and watched the flame dance only to one side. It bent and straightened, bent and straightened in a rhythm. *Move, move, move*, it seemed to say. She leaned over the flame and heated the bottom of the pipe, taking the smoke deep into her lungs and exhaling. Her head felt as if it were being pulled down but her eyes rolled upward to rest on Zhèng Yī's name, birth and death dates.

You're not depressed, a voice from deep within her said, *you're hungover.*

She smiled to herself as she recognized the memory of Zhèng Yǐ's counsel. For a moment, she reminisced about the trysts on the flower boat with him. Some nights it was as if she wasn't being paid to be there, but as if they were just a normal couple eating, drinking and enjoying each other. *I miss you, husband.*

Perhaps he was right, she had been indulging every night with Chūntáo for the two-week celebration. They had sent a servant twice to retrieve more rum, plus she had rendered and smoked an entire bottle of blue opium pills. What she was smoking now was the abundant resin in the bottom of the pipe. It was doable high.

Her eyes slipped shut and her head drooped forward as the drug took hold, her body following. She sighed and reveled in the warmth and comfort the opium offered. Soon she was swimming awkwardly, her body folded in a Balasana yoga position. A giggle formed in her throat as she realized there were other creatures in the water with her; they looked like sea cows. Happy, content faces smiled at her as they swam by, their warm, sweet and almost dog-like faces seemed to offer her some type of peace or calm. She took a deep breath in and—

"Zhèng de Guǎfù, are you well?"

Mógū began to gasp for air as her senses returned to her; she slid the opium pipe into the folds of her clothes hoping the young woman hadn't seen it. She was still on the ground in front of Zhèng Yǐ's shrine. The woman talking to her was a distant cousin in the Zhèng family. Mógū knew she was here to honor her husband who had been killed at the Battle of Tiger's Mouth. The widow was carrying a bunch of yellow flowers and her eyes were red rimmed. Fully aware of her surroundings now, Mógū reached into her pocket and took out a few gold coins and set them on the small offering plate.

"I'm fine, thank you," she mumbled, knowing her voice sounded groggy. She rose and left the small temple giving the young woman her privacy. As she walked back to the house an idea began to form in her head, one of happiness, marriage, wealth and independence.

Chapter Thirty-Seven – Po Tsai's Return

After the spring equinox, Mógū began each day on the rock ledge overlooking the harbor and bay. It was the spot where she and Po Tsai had sat the night before he left. Sometimes she pictured the hundreds of blacks on the shore, the orange dots of their fires and the sounds of their songs. She wondered if Po Tsai had gotten them home. For a brief panic-stricken moment, she wondered what she would do if he returned with his boat still full of humans.

The sun rose at her back, the warmth comforting. They had just returned from their tax run and there was some activity at the docks. She watched as the crew unloaded boxes of food and ammunition. There was one crate that had been painted ornately bright green. It was the correspondence delivery crate. The idea had caught on so quickly that they needed a larger system for sorting and delivering the small parcels. She knew inside the green crate there were smaller wooden boxes labeled with each stop. There was a slot cut on the top of each box for efficient sorting.

When their junk would pull into the harbor, two men would take the crate off the boat. Usually there would already be a line of people waiting to pick up their letters and drop off new ones. One of the men would take the small box labeled with the village's name and open it, calling out the names on the front. The other man would collect the fees and outgoing letters. He would then insert them into the appropriate stop's box. The smaller boxes fit snuggly back into the crate and when it was time to leave again, they would carry it back aboard. There were chicken, egg and pig crates painted the same color. When they collected fowl or swine instead of coin, they were kept in these separate crates. It made Mógū proud how the idea had caught on and created more profits.

She took a sip of her jasmine tea and breathed in the fragrance of it combined with the tree blossoms. A shadow on the horizon caught her attention. She pulled her spy glass from her sash and brought it to her eye. The boats were big with several smaller ones in formation in front and flanked on the sides. She held the looking glass directed at the sails of one of the bigger junks.

It was Po Tsai. The Red Flags flying on every mast. A grin spread across her face as a mixture of relief and anxiety knotted in her stomach. She stood and glanced back down at the docks. Sunlight streamed over the bluff and created long morning shadows. There was even more activity than only moments before. Everyone should be awake now, she thought as she made her way back to the house. She needed to let Wu Jun and Měiyīng know about the celebration feast for tonight. Chūntáo would need to get up to help with the boys. They would need to bathe and eat breakfast; with little warning Mógū's day became hectic.

Eventually she made her way to the docks. There was excitement among the village. A few men shouted at her and pointed to Po Tsai's fleet which now loomed large in the entrance of the bay. She smiled and waved without comment. She wanted her small fleet of junks moved so Po Tsai's could come in to the main unloading dock. It was clear the crew were already a step ahead of her; the large junk had already been prepped to launch, sails at half-mast, it waited for the shove-off from the wharf. Mógū saw one of her quartermasters, and turned towards him.

"Good morning, Zhèng de Guǎfù," he said, "I believe Captain Cheung Po Tsai has returned."

"I see that," Mógū answered with a sarcastic grin.

"We'll move these boats to the north side of the harbor to make way for Po Tsai and his crew to dock here."

"I should have thought of that," she chuckled, "brilliant idea."

"Thank you, madam," he replied although it sounded like a bit of a question.

The sails snapped up and the big junk began to pull away from the dock. She heard the splash rhythm of the oars as she brought her spy glass to her eye. There was always a possibility Po Tsai was not onboard. The sea was the ultimate warrior, taking whoever she pleased.

She put her spy glass to her eye and scanned the approaching vessels. There was always a possibility of mutiny too, a battle with the Portuguese or Brits. For whatever she knew, the Qīng dynasty could have interrupted Po Tsai's humanitarian voyage. But no, there he was standing on the bow of the front ship commanding the fleet as any quality captain would do.

He made a motion that indicated he had seen her and she acknowledged. She decided she would not let him know how relieved she was he was home in one piece nor would she indicate she had missed him. Consciously her expression became one of indifference. She barked an order to one of the dockhands more as a show of control than it warranted.

"Well someone I know is certainly getting laid tonight," Mógū heard Chūntáo and turned towards her.

"You have a date?" Mógū shot back.

Chūntáo made a face and rolled her eyes. Yīngshí and Xióngshí were following dressed in their finest *hanfus*, their hair had been fashioned in braids in the traditional warrior style. Yīngshí walked with the confidence of a young man whereas Xióngshí still had the gait of a child.

"I'm looking forward to hearing about brother Po Tsai's adventures," Yīngshí said to Mógū as they approached, "I'm sure he has seen parts of the world we may never."

"You will see whatever parts of this world you wish, my son," Mógū said as she cast her arms around their shoulders. Her love for the two of them swelled in her chest, *as long as I'm living, you may have anything you want*, she thought with a smug smile.

The boys continued to showcase their ages, Yīngshí pulled away and stood tall as Xióngshí leaned into his mother. The boy wrapped his arms around Mógū's waist and the four of them stood and waited for Po Tsai's junk to dock.

"Did you miss good ole Po the kid?" Chūntáo asked.

Before Mógū could respond, both boys answered in unison, "Yes."

Mógū's eyes flitted to Chūntáo's. She could feel the mirth bubbling up in her throat. Without saying anything, she shrugged and turned her attention back to the oncoming junk.

"You did," Chūntáo teased. Po Tsai had appeared on the deck and both boys were waving at them, Xióngshí a little more exuberant than his older brother. A flood of emotions from relief to exhilaration washed over Mógū. Perhaps she *had* missed him a bit more than she was willing to admit. "For the record," Chūntáo said, "I didn't."

Chapter Thirty-Eight – It's Just Business

Within days, life had taken on an air of business as usual. Mógū got glimpses of Po Tsai as he went about unloading and cataloging the spoils of his voyage. In front of the boys and Chūntáo, Po Tsai had seemed cordial and friendly. Mógū had hoped to get him alone so they could talk about their wedding and implement her plans for the future. He avoided her at every opportunity.

Before dawn on the third morning, Mógū heard Po Tsai preparing for his day. She slipped across the hallway and into his room without knocking.

"Hey!" he shouted.

"Sshhh, everyone is still asleep," she was full of apprehension.

"What do you want?" his tone was sharp, unfriendly.

"I..." her words caught in her throat, *I missed you. No. I'm happy to see you. No. I'm ready to start our lives together, no, no, no.*

There was a long and awkward silence between them. She broke eye contact first. Her eyes darted around the room and landed on several pieces of wood lying near his travel bags. "Cork?" she asked, the word sounding too loud and too informal.

"Baobab," he answered, "from Madagascar. That's where we docked. The people were not from there, they were from Senegambia."

"Is that far?"

"Yes," he said, his face becoming animated. She could see a glimpse of the Po Tsai she had missed. He retrieved a map and unrolled it on the table in the center of the room. She moved away from the door and joined him. The excitement bubbled from him as he pointed to the map. "We landed here, but most the people were from here and here." He pointed to different towns on the map. "My fear is all those people will be caught and marched right back to the next slave trade ship before they can make their way home. The Brits and French there are worse than the Portuguese here."

"Oh, that reminds me. Did you know Miguel José is dead?"

"Really?" There was a combination of relief and query spread over his face. "Do you know for a fact or is it rumor?"

"I saw his death certificate."

"Well then I'm sure he is dead."

"He is. I killed him."

"What? When? Where?"

"Well, I didn't exactly kill him, he killed himself after we defeated his navy. I sent him home with a message to Mad Maria and needless to say, he was too embarrassed to deliver it."

"Well done," he said with a nod.

"Thank you," she answered, "Po Tsai, I need to… we need to talk about—"

"The wood," he said as he picked up one of the smaller pieces and handed it to her. It was very light and felt like cork but was a deeper red color, not resembling cork at all. "This wood is amazing, it doesn't burn. It's too soft to build from but you can make rope from it, sturdy, strong rope. And fabric too." He prattled on with nervous energy.

Mógū moved around the table and took his hands in hers. "Look at me, Po Tsai. What's going on? You're acting so unusual."

"The wedding, we need to review the terms." His tone lacked emotion. "I don't want to be settled down to only one lover but my loyalty to Zhèng Yī," he said as their eyes met, "my loyalty to you—"

"You're the only one I trust," she interrupted. "A wise man once told me love was—"

"Overrated," he interjected, shaking his head. "Ya, ya, woman, you've reminded me of that before. Sheesh. Get over it."

"Well," she stumbled on her words now, his interruption throwing her off, "going into this union, I'm going to... I'll have to..." He gave her a hard stare, one eyebrow cocked, "agree with you," she spluttered.

"Business is business," he said and gave her a little smile, "I'm not going to demand half like you did but I want the fleet and men that just returned from Africa." She nodded. "As for the tax runs, it would be nice for that to continue to fund my travels."

"I'm going in a little different direction," she began as they moved to wooden chairs in front of a small, dark mahogany table, "the correspondence delivery system we've created seems to be quite prosperous and above board," she said, "I want amnesty from Youngyan."

"Amnesty?" he choked, "what for?"

"I received news the Green Flags have already surrendered to the Dynasty. We will be in a good position to negotiate." She could tell she had his attention. "I want to operate my delivery system and finish raising my sons. I don't want the pirate life for Yīngshí and Xióngshí," she said, "they need to make an honest living, be businessmen or politicians."

"Politicians? I thought you said an honest living."

"You know what I mean. I don't want them to have to wield their swords, Xióngshí has a peaceful soul and Yīngshí is such a compassionate, intelligent young man."

"That doesn't have anything to do with me," he answered, "I love Zhèng Yǐ's sons like my own but—"

"I have every intention on acquiring an officer's position in the Qīng Navy for you and you would be able to explore under their flag and protection." She had already given thought to using Po Tsai's leadership skills as a leverage in her negotiations with the seventh Manchu emperor.

The look he was giving her was somewhere between optimism and the condescending way she looked at her sons when they proposed something outrageous.

"You get me a captain's position in the Chinese Navy and I'll be your groom," he answered with a laugh, "you certainly know how to get my attention.

"If I keep the delivery system, I can still procure the things that make my quality of life so fine."

"Blue beads," he answered.

"And fine Caribbean rum," she said with a smile, "we'll settle for nothing less than amnesty for everyone, a captain's position for you and a whorehouse for me."

"Sounds like the perfect career choices for us." They rose and moved towards the door. "Zhèng Yī will always have my loyalty. *You* will always have my loyalty." The love they both had for Zhèng Yī seemed to ricochet between them. "Just know, I'm leaving again," he said, breaking the silence between them, "and there may be another lover in my life, you need to know that too."

"There may be one in my life too." She smiled.

"There's not," he said with a wink and turned away, "if you'll excuse me, I have things to get done today."

"Of course," she answered and left him with his baobab wood and maps.

Chapter Thirty-Nine – Denied

Mógū continued her day to day life as if nothing had changed, but everything was changing around her. Another notorious band of pirates had surrendered to the Dynasty and the Portuguese were uniting with the Brits to seize Lantau Island. She could hear the battles if not see them.

"I will not surrender," she told Po Tsai one evening after their dinner, "it's like these men are rolling over as if they are stray dogs looking for shelter." She took a sip of her rum.

"Did you send the correspondence to Youngyan?" Po Tsai asked. She nodded. The letter she had put together looked official with her terms defined and the red wax seal on the back. In the beginning of it, she noted how beneficial it would be if Po Tsai were a leader for the official Qīng Navy. Furthermore, it would be advantageous for everyone if she were no longer traversing the waters. She had asked for the large junk to continue her route, amnesty for all twenty-five thousand of her warriors, and a proper business for her to run while in her latter life. A legitimate business that would also offer services and amenities for the men of his country.

Life continued. There were rumors the Portuguese would battle the Brits to take control of Lantau Island if their demands weren't met. Mógū was certain the Qīng Dynasty would put up a fight before letting it go to their adversary. Plans for battle on what she considered her territory caused anxiety. She looked forward to hearing from the Dynasty so her life could once more have a definite direction.

Youngyan's reply finally arrived via personal messenger after several weeks of an agonizing wait.

Zhèng de Guǎfù,

We received your correspondence but will have to cordially deny your requests. Although Cheung Po Tsai is indeed a warrior and leader, it would not benefit us to have a criminal killer among our ranks nor be wise to give a known opium trader a large boat to continue to profit from an item that legalization is nearing its end.

Amnesty for such a large group of lawbreakers will also have to be denied. You must understand, there are just too many offenders to accommodate. These men shall be punished for their crimes individually.

As for you and your sons, there is a whorehouse in Macau that may be suitable to your needs. The price is fair. Purchase could be arranged. Due to Zhèng Yǐ's family ties and their allies, amnesty for you and your immediate family may be settled upon once your band has surrendered and sentences for them served.

It is not in the Dynasty's best interest to bend to the whims of known outlaws. To avoid further loss of life, my best recommendation for you is to accept our generous offer and advise your men of the steps of surrender. There is nothing more to discuss.

Mógū's jaw tightened as she read the valediction, 'Cordially Yours.' Youngyan's signature glared up at her, it seemed too big for the page it was penned on. She lifted her eyes to the messenger who stood at attention near the door.

"You may leave," she glared at the young man.

"Madam Zhèng, no reply?" Mógū could see he was uncomfortable. His eyes darted all around the room, careful not to catch hers. What had Youngyan expected? For her to cow down to this messenger, this… boy? She slowly walked towards him, her brow folded into a concerned scowl.

"No," she said as she stood in front of him.

"No to which part, Zhèng de Guǎfù?" his eyes had ceased to rove around the room and rested at a point over the top of her head. His expression now was alert, he stood at attention.

"All of it," she snapped, "you go back and tell Youngyan I will personally slit his throat before I alter my specifications." She took in a deep breath and continued, "First, I'll bleed out King George and Mad Maria, then I'll come for China. Tell your coward of a leader he should be honored to have a man such as Cheung Po Tsai serving under him, furthermore, I'm not looking to buy a brothel, it shall be gifted to me, with my junk." The young man nodded and she heard the slightest intake of breath. "All my men shall have amnesty too; this deal is all or nothing. Can you remember all of that?" He nodded. "You're dismissed." She turned on her heel and began to shred the message as she marched back into her chamber. There was a light rap on the door. Mógū prepared to berate the messenger, was he dense? What was it he didn't understand?

Chūntáo's head popped into the room, she hadn't waited for Mógū to reach the door.

"No go, huh?" she asked as she stepped across the threshold.

"The man is an idiot," she sighed.

"He was just a boy doing his job, sister."

"Not the messenger, Youngyan." Mógū rolled her eyes.

"Beggars can't be choosers," Chūntáo replied.

Rage roiled off Mógū. "I'm not a beggar," she snapped, "I am a pirate. I am the dragon of The South Seas and I will not be denied, nor will my men."

Chapter Forty – Move It

Mógū tried to read as much as she could about the political standpoint of the Dynasty. In daily periodicals that Chūntáo brought her, she learned another band of bandits had succumbed to the pressures put on them by the Chinese government and had surrendered.

It was predicted the Brits would be the victors over Lantau as they had sent significantly more ships to defend the rock island. As Mógū read the article regarding the logistics the Brits would be up against, Chūntáo interrupted her thoughts. "Maybe you should consider moving the booty."

"To where?" Mógū mumbled and continued to read.

"Huê, of course. We could pay someone to watch over it, know it's safe. I don't trust George the third or any of his men. They are all as mad as Maria."

Mógū didn't acknowledge it was a good idea nor did she vocalize she had already been thinking of the loot stashed deep in the Lantau Island cave. She gave Chūntáo a reassuring shrug and continued to delve into the paper's newsworthy stories.

One article debated which European country would be better off taking over; Portugal who already had a presence in Macau or the British who would then be the second European country to take an interest in the area. It was long known that the English had created a trading port in India. The new company that was emerging was known as the East India Company and flew under King George III's flag, but was basically owned and operated by the citizens of India. They consistently traded slaves, cotton, indigo dye, saltpeter for gunpowder, salt, pepper and other spices as well as opium.

She wondered how difficult it would be to get their loot from the cave, load it onto the junks then sail it to Huê and stash it without a confrontation; without any bloodshed. If they sailed to Lantau when the moon was a waning sliver, they could move through the darkness to the cave and be loaded and aweigh before sun-up. The more men she could take, the more likely they could get everything in one trip. It would no longer matter if the men knew where the stash was if it were being moved. Which lead to another question, moved where?

Later that night, Mógū sought out Po Tsai and expressed her concern about Lantau Island.

He nodded. "I hate to admit you're right, but indeed, you are. I've given thought myself about where to move the loot. I highly doubt the Brits would find it but once they have settled, it will be harder to get to."

"There are two large caves in Huê," she said, "there are a number of loyal men there too. We could hire them as guards."

"Loyal enough to kill for you?" he asked with one eyebrow cocked.

"I would say yes," she replied thinking of the merchants and men she had done business with in Huê. Yes, that was the answer, move the booty to Huê in Dai Nam before the British took over the island.

Less than a week later, as a slice of moon sank in the western sky, Mógū and approximately five thousand men set off in four junks to the island. They set up to keep the task efficient and as quiet as possible. The men made a long line from the beach to the cave where they handed over items from one man to the next, to the next, to the next down the line and back to the small boats that had been launched off the larger junks. When one boat was filled, it would launch back to unload on one of the junks and another small boat would take its place.

The firearms and boxes of ammunition required a cart pulled by a muzzled donkey and was slower than the smaller items being transported. Looking at the stars, Mógū realized there was only about an hour left before daylight. She made her way to the cave to see what was still there and was pleasantly surprised the majority of the booty had been moved without incident.

In a low voice she advised the men to head back to the junks. She exited the cave and moved the rocks and brush back over the opening to conceal it. She moved quietly through the low climbing brush and made her way back to the beach. She watched the men as they loaded the rest of the loot.

While waiting for them to finish, she wandered down the beach. There was an outline of several small boats pulled up on the shore. Curious, she moved further upland into the shadows. She could see there was a larger ship buoyed in the deeper waters. She was sure it hadn't been there before. The idea they had pulled these smaller ships up on the beach and made camp while she and her crew moved the booty raised the hair on the back of her neck.

Chapter Forty-One – A British Boat

Once everyone and everything was loaded and secured Mógū sought out Po Tsai. "Did you see the other ship?"

He shrugged. "There's a natural lee on the other side of those rocks so it would make sense if someone was going to moor and embark onto the island that would be the logical place to do it."

"Do we know who it is?"

"My best guess is the Brits. We sent a few scouts out and it appears like an exploring surveyor crew. Harmless."

"We should take their boat."

"We're not really prepared for a battle. Besides, the junks are loaded to the max."

"The small boats along the shoreline suggest the men are on the land."

She could see he was pondering the idea.

"Usually there are a few men left on board."

"Yes, but we have the element of surprise and we're definitely prepared for hand to hand combat. Our men are always ready for that." He nodded and she set the plan into motion.

She had the crew lower a small dingy. She took four men and they moved towards the looming British ship. They were able to board through a gunner window on one of the lower decks. The men began to pull up the anchor, the wheel of the apparatus seeming loud in the pre-dawn hour. With stealth she moved to the next deck up. The narrow hallway was lined with doors she assumed went into individual bunkers for the sailors. She turned one of the handles and peered in. She was right, the small room had two bunk beds and nothing much more.

Once she was on the next deck up, one of the men came to her and told her they had successfully raised the anchor and attached a tow rope to Po Tsai's ship.

"I'm not sure the men's backs will be strong enough to row both ships," he said, "I think I'll raise the smallest sail and catch some of the early morning breeze. That may help."

"Good idea," she agreed.

A commotion startled them both. Four white men began to shout, their panic apparent in their tone. One man had a pistol and was holding it aimed at them. She could see he was not a warrior; his hand shook and the gun was not pointed at the right angle. Mógū's man moved with the quickness of predator and slayed the man with his blade. The other three yipped and huddled together with wide, terrified eyes but didn't make another noise. Three more white men appeared from the sleeping quarters. One with an overly large mustache seemed to assess the situation in an instant. He yelled and motioned towards the dead man. Mógū drew her cutlass and began to move towards him.

The man's demeanor quickly diminished. He held up his hands. Water brimmed at his eyes, he was talking fast in a language she couldn't understand but clearly, he was upset about the death of the man with the pistol. The other men of her crew had joined them, each with their weapons drawn. The man continued in his staccato speech, arms high over his head, he began to walk towards the stairs that led back to the hall of chamber doors.

"Hey!" she yelled. He stopped and motioned for her to follow him. He then turned a circle with his hands still above his head. She looked at her men who were equally as confused.

The boat jerked slightly as the tow ropes slack was picked up. The man stumbled towards the open stairwell. He lowered his hands to catch himself. Mógū looked to the others. The white men were huddled together. Only one looked anything but terrified. The boat jerked again.

"Raise that sail," she barked. It was almost dawn; the breeze was picking up. She saw all the sails were raised on the junk that was pulling them. "You two, keep your swords at their throats," she motioned to the small group of men. "I'm going to check out whatever it is this man wants me to see." She heard the uniform intake of breath as her men moved closer to their captives, then the snap of the sail as it caught its first gust of wind. The tow rope jerks continued but not as severe.

Mógū followed the man to his quarters. His room was bigger than the ones she had poked her head into. It had only one bed and a large desk. Several leather-bound books were lined up neatly on a shelf with a dowel fashioned across them so they didn't tumble off in rough waters. The man continued to prattle in his native tongue. He snatched a large book from the desk and opened it pointing to the drawings inside. She motioned for him to put it back on the desk, he did and she moved closer. The man lit a lantern with flint. He hadn't stopped talking the entire time.

She studied the drawing and realized it was a sketch of Lantau Island from a distance. She turned the page and saw another drawing, this one of a pulley system. A few pages more she saw a sketch of an Apocynaceae tree, the tubers and flowers specifically. Another page showed the full tree in each season. The language he was spouting was etched across every page horizontally.

She raised her hand for him to stop speaking. Finally, he did. She thumbed through more pages to see sea animals, birds and insects also drawn with great detail. He began to talk again and moved towards her pointing to the pages. Mógū drew out her cutlass.

"NO!" the man screamed and dropped to his knees on the floor. He pulled his arms over his head and started to softly cry. She turned the weapon and patted his back with the flat side. He raised his head and she motioned towards the door. He scrambled to his feet and exited the room with her behind him.

She saw the junk had quit rowing and the tether was released.

"We're going to sail this beast home," one of the men said to her, "it's too much for our row squad. Our prisoners are more than happy to help us, aren't you fellas?" He laughed. The British men were each doing a different task getting the ship up and under its own power.

She looked back to the shore line and marveled how accurate the white man's sketch had been. She couldn't help but wonder if the men on the shore had woken up and discovered their ship missing. Perhaps they would think these men had abandoned their flag.

Chapter Forty-Two – Quick Stop at Home

By the time they reached their own harbor, the white men had been tied at their wrists then attached together in a line. Mógū had searched the ship for more men but found none. She did find crates of opium pills and piles of British silver as well as pepper pods and what appeared to be salt but it was finer and sweeter. There was little to no weaponry or ammunition but several kegs of beer and a dozen cases of red wine in corked glass bottles.

Only the British ship docked. The three large junks stayed out in the delta. She needed to accompany them to Huê to secure the booty in the caves there, but first she needed to deal with these British men and this ship.

As she disembarked, she heard Yīngshí's voice shout, "Mother!"

"Are you alright? What are you doing here, son?" she scanned the docks for Chūntáo.

"Youngyan's runner is here. He arrived yesterday with another letter."

The white men were being led off the ship. The man with the mustache was bringing up the rear. She marched over to them and drew out her cutlass. With a quick, effortless stroke, she cut the rope between the mustached man and the one in front of him. She bent and grabbed the end of the rope and handed it to Yīngshí.

"Let's go," she said and motioned with her cutlass for the man to follow her son. He glanced nervously over his shoulder at the others who were being led in a different direction.

As soon as they reached the big house, Mógū saw the messenger. He was standing near the door, his eyes and shoulders drooped from exhaustion.

"Has he been standing here all night?" she asked.

"Yeah," Yīngshí replied, "Chūntáo called him the devil's delivery dāizi and told him to stay put."

"Where did she come up with that?" she shook her head with a grin and approached the lad. He saw the white man being led by the child and his face knit into confusion, then a flash of fear as he saw Mógū's cutlass. He fumbled in his satchel and retrieved the stationery.

Zhèng de Guǎfù,

Foolish woman. Due to the fact you did not accept my most generous offer, you and your men have no choice but to surrender. If you do not, our navy, teamed up with the British Crown Navy, will not rest until every last one of your men are dead. Other bands of bandits are ceding every day. There is no shame in surrendering.

She didn't finish reading it. "No! No! NO!" she screamed, as she ripped the letter into two then four pieces. She glared at the messenger. "Tell Youngyan he is the fool. My original offer is the only one I will accept." She held up her thumb. "Naval position for Po Tsai," —her first finger popped up—"amnesty for all my men. Every single one!" —the second finger joined the first—"a whore house free and clear of any encumbering mortgage, and," —she raised her third finger—"a boat." Her breathing resumed to normal. "I've recently come into possession of a delightful British craft." She forced a fake smile. "You tell him if he doesn't have a spare for me, I'll keep this one, in fact, tell that scoundrel I'll write to King George himself and tell him I had no choice but to execute these men because Youngyan is too damn stubborn to meet my needs. Do you understand?"

The messenger nodded. "Who are the men you're going to execute?" he managed to ask as he fumbled for a piece of parchment and quill. She watched him struggle to get into a position to make notes. Aggravated, she snatched the quill from his hand and handed it to the white man on the tether then pointed to the parchment. He looked as confused as the messenger boy.

"Write your names," she said but the white man couldn't understand her. She poked him in his chest with her index finger then pointed to the parchment again. After a moment's thought he slowly nodded and with his hands still bound wrote horizontally across the page left to right, Richard Glasspoole.

Once he was finished, he tried to hand the quill back to the messenger, but Mógū shook her head and made a circle motion with her finger then pointed back to the parchment. The man looked confused. She pointed to the harbor then to the place he had just written his name. Slowly, understanding dawned on his face and he wrote the other five men's names under his. Once he was done, he handed the quill back to the boy who was studying the unfamiliar script.

After a moment of complete motionless silence, Mógū waved her hands as if she were shooing chickens. "Go, go!" As he left, the front door of the house opened and Chūntáo came bouncing down the stairs.

"Hello, sister." She glanced at the man on the tether. "New pet?" she asked Yīngshí. A bubble of nervous laughter escaped his lips. "Wu Jun heard you were back and said if you want some food, she's got breakfast ready." She turned to the man and arched her hand towards him like a cat's claw. "Rawr, rawr."

"I really should get back to the docks. I'm going to Huê with Po Tsai," Mógū said.

"You've got time to eat, c'mon," Chūntáo replied and started up the steps heading back into the house. Yīngshí followed and the man on the leash had no choice but to keep up. Mógū sighed and went in too. She could hear her youngest son yammering on about something as they approached the kitchen. As soon as Xióngshí saw his older brother leading a full-grown white man on a leash, he stopped speaking, his mouth hung slack for a moment. Měiyīng was preparing the noodles and bone broth and stopped in her tracks when she saw the guest.

"Good morning," Wu Jun said and placed another setting at the table without missing a beat. Mógū put her cutlass back in the scabbard at her waist and untied the man's hands. He sat at the table, eyes wide, with an expression of fear mixed with confusion. The boys were seated and eagerly waiting for their morning meal.

"I haven't much time, we're going to Huê," Mógū said.

"I doubt you'll leave today, you just got here," Wu Jun answered.

Měiyīng served everyone then sat and began to eat, her eyes darting from one person to the other.

"I'll pet sit if you'd like," Chūntáo said and winked at the man who hadn't touched his food. "Eat," she told him and motioned to his food. He looked to Mógū who was eating fast. Her chop sticks dunked in and out of the broth expertly bringing out noodles and chunks of pork.

"I want to go to Huê," Yīngshí said, "can I, Mother?"

She shook her head. "Not this trip, son, maybe next time." Mógū looked at the man. He hadn't eaten. "We've got to go, eat," she said. When he didn't make a move towards the food, she picked up the rope from the floor and made a motion towards the door with it. The urgency finally registered and he picked up the bowl with both hands and drank it down. Some of the fluid and noodles fell onto his shirt. He set the bowl down and looked around at the dozen eyes watching him then he gave a little grin and burped.

"Mother!" Xióngshí exclaimed, eyes wide, "that's bad manners to slurp your soup like that. Why did he do that?"

Chūntáo and Yīngshí were laughing, even Měiyīng stifled a grin. Mógū rolled her eyes. "Let's go," she said and reattached the rope to the man's wrists.

Chapter Forty-Three – A New Hiding Place

Moving the treasure to Huê proved to be a more difficult task than Mógū had expected. They had thousands of men helping them move everything from the cave on Lantau Island but she dared not disclose the new hiding spot to everyone. That left her the six British men, a couple dozen well-trusted men of her crew, and four donkeys.

Because of the high number of people that they had taken to remove the loot from the Lantau cave they were able to reload everything into two of the large junks with a limited crew and it all fit. They launched to do their regular Dai Nam protection tax run and correspondence delivery with the two junks full of loot, the others as business-as-usual presence and some added protection.

When they got to Huê they stayed the night in the harbor using the excuse that Mógū had an early morning appointment with one of the banking merchants. They waited until sundown and loaded one of the smaller junks with two donkeys, two carts and as much of the loot as could be carried.

Once those two carts were loaded, Mógū accompanied the first load to the cave. She had left explicit instructions the junk was to return to the large junk and wait until they gave a signal from the shore to return with the other two carts and more of the loot. The junks would be easier to defend if they stayed in the harbor.

The cave access was considerably more difficult to get to than the Lantau one. The pitch blackness of the night added another level of challenge. The British men seemed to revel in the challenge of getting the trail safe enough for carts to traverse over without rolling.

The man she had hired to assist her assured her they were getting close. He pointed up to the opening, it was close but almost straight up. Mógū stopped the donkey caravan and drew out her cutlass and began to whack the bamboo and other flora making a pathway. She heard the British artist man's voice behind her, she stopped cutting and turned to him, her cutlass on the ready.

The man had retrieved from one of the carts a long, thick piece of the baobab tree rope Po Tsai had made. He secured one end to a massive rock and then motioned for Mógū to follow him. He ducked low and began to move through the trees and climbed upwards to the opening of the cave. Mógū followed holding the torch as high as she dared. Once they had reached the mouth of the cave, the man looped the rope around a rather large tree and started to move back down. Mógū was confused and a bit irritated at him. They had climbed all that way and they didn't go in the cave.

The man took the rope from the rock and looped it around another tree and tied it to the end that was looped at the top. When he pulled it taut the majority of the branches lifted and opened up an area where the carts could pass. With excitement he moved to the donkey attached to the first cart. He pointed to the leather hitch and metal ring holding the two together then he pointed to the rope. Mógū realized he wanted to attach the hitch to the rope, she gave him a nervous smile. He took that as an invitation and moved the donkey in place and used the metal o-ring to attach the donkey's cart to the rope then began to pull the donkey from the front. Surprisingly, it followed the man up the narrow, rocky traverse.

Mógū moved quickly past the man and the donkey and reached the top where the cave opened. She went in and held the torch high. The cave was large with two openings going in opposite directions.

She wandered a little way down the one to the left but it got quite narrow rather quickly. With haste she returned and went down the passageway to the right. It turned almost ninety degrees but then opened into another larger room. She smiled knowing how easy it would be to close off the corridor once the booty was safely stored.

The donkey cart had crested the opening. The men all looked surprised and exhausted. This was only a small fraction of what needed to be hauled into the cave. It was going to be a long night. They secured the two carts in the front part of the cave.

"Take the donkeys back down to get the next two carts," she said to one of her men. "By the time you get back, these will be empty and ready for round two. If you can, bring all four donkeys and four carts as full as you can safely pack them."

The crewman nodded. "Should I take the *gweilos* too?" he asked.

She shook her head. "No, leave them, I'll have them unload the cart. Take the men who are armed and ready to fight if necessary."

He nodded and cried out some orders to the men and they all turned to follow him out of the cave.

"No, not you," Mógū yelled to the Brits. Her words were harsher than she meant them to be and the cave echoed with her authority. "Hey!"

The white men looked around confused and Mógū motioned with her cutlass to the loaded carts then motioned to the opening on the right. They understood and moved to start unloading.

Mógū had brought two other torches. She went into the second cave and searched for someplace to attach one to the wall. There was the perfect divot about halfway into the cavern. She shoved the unlit torch into it then took her lit torch and set the second one ablaze. The light it cast seemed to soften the white men's faces.

As daybreak crested the horizon, they had moved eight cartloads of plunder, only about half of one of the junks. Conveniently, when the rope was removed, the plants all snapped back to where they were before, making the opening of the cave virtually impossible to see. She was pleased with that aspect of the new hiding place, but the pace of moving everything was a burden.

"Let's go to Ha Long Bay as scheduled but make another overnight stop on our way back," she told the quartermaster once she returned to the junk with the Brits, donkeys and empty carts. A job she estimated would only take a few days turned into a few weeks' worth of effort.

The protection tax was getting more and more difficult to collect. At times her men had to take the money by force or if a particular village refused to pay, one of her men would kill the merchant who refused to hand over their payment. It was rumored the emperor Nguyên Anh had been negotiating a deal with the Qīng Dynasty which involved Laos and Cambodia. If they were to come to an amicable alliance, she was sure Nguyên Anh would send warriors to stop them from fleecing his constituents. She would collect as long as she could and increase her delivery system prices. Certainly, Nguyên Anh could see what a service it was to have the correspondence move up and down the coast in a scheduled roster. As the service became more popular, she could see it becoming international on the trade ships going both north and south.

Her main concern now was amicable relations. It would be important to remain harmonious with Emperor Nguyên Anh since she had property in Dai Nam and now all her wealth was being stored there too. Yes, perhaps she would include a payment to Youngyan from Nguyên Anh's people on her next round of negotiations.

Chapter Forty-Four – Sketches

Two full moons passed without Youngyan's messenger returning. There was resistance at every port for the protection tax. Some were saying it was nothing more than extortion. Since the Dynasty hadn't struck the shores of Dai Nam, she would argue it was indeed an obligatory fee. At the bigger ports military forces were positioned at the docks. Mógū's people were allowed to exchange the correspondence but often were told only two crew members could disembark.

Sometimes, she would threaten them and carry on with her business. "Do you know who I am?" she would snap. Occasionally that worked, other times it turned into a bother. A small tussle broke out at one of the ports resulting in six men dead; two were from Mógū's crew. Before they left, she got her money.

"Tell Nguyên Anh that was unnecessary bloodshed," she barked at one of the martial men, as some of her crewmen retrieved the bodies of the fallen. "What we had here today is nothing in comparison to what Youngyan's men will do to this puny port if the payments are missed." She started to walk away then turned and added, "Or what my crew will do next time if the money is not here in a timely manner. Do you understand?" she screamed.

The young man nodded and bowed then backed away.

In addition to the transformations along the coast of Dai Nam, Mógū was concerned about the changes happening across the bay from He On Kong. She had read in a monthly periodical that the Dynasty had negotiated with the British and part of their concession was the big rock island as a settlement. It was bothersome that the Brits were there and the Portuguese in Macau. The Europeans were getting too cozy. It wasn't enough that her booty was safely stashed in Huê, but the island itself was being established by the British.

Every day she would see more of the big ships with the red, white and blue flags. She sent several of the small junks armed to the hilt with hundreds of men to just be a presence along the shores. It didn't appear to be a deterrent, in fact, it appeared like more and more ships showed up regardless of how many red flags were flying.

"It's a matter of time before those pompous white bastards will be stealing He On Kong from us," Po Tsai said one early morning while they were scouting the British goings-on. Just before dawn, they had taken a small vessel across the bay to see what the Brits were building.

"We'll rise and fight before I hand over my homeland," she replied.

"It will be a short battle if Youngyan and King George join forces." She shook her head and took out her spy glass. Po Tsai continued, "Perhaps Chūntáo and the boys should move to the bamboo house in Huê."

Mógū was only half listening as she concentrated, squinting her eye to get a better look. There was a pulley system similar to the one she had seen in Richard Glasspoole's sketch book. Large baskets were suspended to the cable. She focused through the lenses and realized the baskets and rope were made from metal. The white men strapped large pieces of lumber to the open-ended containers. A team of horses were attached to a circular configuration and when prompted to move forward, the strength of the horses moved the apparatus as it hauled the long towline upward. As she studied the terrain, she realized how genius the contraption was; there would be no way to move donkeys or horses up the steep crag, especially if they were dragging large pieces of wood.

These foreigners clearly didn't know six of their own countrymen were being held in a storage cellar so close to where they were constructing their new building.

"It looks like a small temple," Mógū said to Po Tsai when she got her first view of the structure on the top of the hill.

"Probably Christian," Po Tsai agreed. For decades the Europeans had been sending Christian missionaries to these waters looking to convert the weak. It would not be a surprise to anyone if they were constructing a temple to worship their new-aged god.

As the day ramped up, Mógū and Po Tsai made their way back to their safe haven. She watched the activity on the shore as they approached. So many families to worry about, to keep safe and fed. Uncertainty nagged at Mógū's soul.

"I'm serious about moving the boys to Dai Nam." Po Tsai brought up the subject again as they neared their docks. "You too. I could wait here for Youngyan's messenger."

Mógū shook her head. "I'm going to wait it out," she said firmly, "if the others want to go, certainly they—"

"You may not have a choice," he argued, cutting her off, "it could come down to hand to hand combat."

"Well then, we'll have to be sure we're ready," Mógū answered as she scanned the populace working the docks. There were a lot of people still here, with a little hand to hand combat training, she was sure they could hold their own until she and Youngyan could come to an acceptable arrangement.

The small group of British men were Mógū's main concern. She had insisted they not be treated badly. She knew she was walking a fine line with their well-being. On one hand, they were prisoners but on the other hand, they were pawns in her negotiations. Her intention was to send them home once a satisfactory agreement had been arranged with Nguyên Anh. These men would talk and tell their stories; that was human nature. She needed to ensure a pleasing pretense to those who would hear them. With that in mind, she oversaw their captivity. She made sure they were well fed and had a daily dose of fresh air and exercise.

Mógū had kept the white man's sketch books. Richard Glasspoole's drawings became a little bit of an obsession for her. She looked through them dozens of times, turning the pages leisurely, studying the landscape pictures trying to guess where they had been drawn.

There were other drafts of systems; pulley and cable drawings, sketches of contraptions and what appeared to be formulas to make them work. Foreign letters were scrawled on the edges of the paper with arced arrows pointing this way and that.

On occasion, Mógū would allow the British men to join them for their nightly meal. The dining hall was big enough to accommodate more than a dozen people and none of the British sailors were a threat, in fact, they acted grateful and smiled a lot during these encounters.

On one of these evenings, Yīngshí and Xióngshí were playing mahjong. The men watched them and talked amongst themselves in their native tongue. Mógū had brought one of the smaller sketch books and waved it to get Glasspoole's attention. He gave her a broad smile and joined her at the table.

"Where was this?" she asked speaking slowly, showing him one of the landscape sketches. He launched into a rapid staccato speech she didn't understand. She shook her head and shushed him and turned the page. It was a sketch of six men stretched across the open book. Four were engaged in a conversation sitting at a table. One man was asleep in an oversized chair, the other asleep, splayed out on the floor in front of him. It appeared to be a scene from the boat. She realized the sixth man, the one asleep in the chair, was the one that hadn't survived.

As soon as Richard saw it, he started explaining something else to her, his tone different, somber. She gave him a sympathetic look having no idea what he was saying yet knowing somehow he was talking about the dead man. She gave him a sad smile and turned the next page. Both sides were blank. She gave Glasspoole a little grin and shrugged. He motioned for it, she took a step back and he sat in front of it. From a pocket he produced a charcoal pencil and began to sketch just as Chūntáo and Měiyīng entered with their dinner.

Richard Glasspoole set the book and pencil aside for a few minutes while he ate then returned to it, moving away from the small crowd. Once the boys finished their meals, they returned to the mahjong game.

"Don't cheat," Mógū heard Xióngshí whine.

"I'm not, you're just a bad player," his older brother retorted.

Mógū watched them, her heart full. Such handsome and well-mannered boys they had all raised together. She turned her attention to Chūntáo who was talking with her mouth full to Po Tsai who was clearly not listening. If someone had told her ten years earlier where her life would have ended up, she would have never believed it. The love she has for her children is something one could never imagine; all of her reservations of pregnancy years ago absent.

Dinner was done and Měiyīng bustled about removing the plates and serving bowls. Po Tsai excused himself and left. Chūntáo had a cup of rum she was happily sipping from, she looked lost in her own thoughts. Richard Glasspoole was still drawing and the other white men were talking among themselves.

"I won!" Xióngshí announced joyfully. Mógū's attention turned to her children. Her eye caught Yīngshí's and she knew the older boy had let his little brother take the victory.

"Good job, little man," Chūntáo said extending her arms. Xióngshí ran into them and nuzzled her as she pulled him onto her lap. Mógū rose to help put the mahjong tiles back into the wooden storage box.

"Mommy, look," Xióngshí exclaimed, "it's us!"

Mógū turned to see what her son was so excited about.

On the left, Mógū was surprised to see a fairly accurate depiction of herself on the paper. On the right was a picture of her two sons playing the mahjong game, a smile on Xióngshí's face, a stern scholarly expression on Yīngshí's.

"What a surprise," she said to no one particular. She watched as he put finishing touches on the drawing. When finished, Richard Glasspoole gently tore the picture of the boys playing the game from the book and handed it to her. She felt a rush of love for her offspring. The picture reminded her of the large oil paintings of British, French and Portuguese royals. This simple sketch caused a huge smile inside her heart. Her sons, preserved in their youth on the paper. Xióngshí and Yīngshí gathered around to look at it more closely. Richard began to tear the likeness of Mógū from the book.

"No, no," she said to him and placed her hand on his shaking her head. On the backside of her portrait was the sketch of the dead man, she didn't want the reminder. She gently closed the book and handed it to him.

Again, she thought about the story he would tell once he was a free man, once she was granted amnesty and could let him return to England. It was a lovely rendering of her, Richard had chosen to portray her in her captain's clothes, hair pulled back, sailing hat on her head. Let him show it to King George and Mad Maria, let the world know what she looked like. She certainly didn't look like the fierce fire breathing dragon she had been made out to be. Yes, let him keep it to remember her by.

Richard stood as he accepted the sketch book and bowed towards Mógū before he followed the other men back to their enclosure.

Chapter Forty-Five – Long Overdue Letter

The moon was getting fat again. It had almost been three months since Mógū had sent the messenger back with her denial of Youngyan's offer. From across the bay she watched the British make themselves comfortable. With a sense of dread, she realized time was of the essence. Po Tsai was right, it was only a matter of time before they spread out what they considered was their new domain. She could, and would, stay and fight, but to what end? She and her men could kill the lot of them but there would be more. They would just keep coming.

She needed the counteroffer from the Dynasty to seal her future and everyone else's future. The entire Red Flag Fleet was counting on her. If the offer wasn't favorable, she would stay on He On Kong and fight. It would be best if she sent Chūntáo and her sons to Huê to keep them out of harm's way. Perhaps she should have included He On Kong island in her negotiations too. It was too late for that; she could only hope Youngyan would see things her way and grant her and her men amnesty.

As the days passed, she knew many decisions would have to be made soon. She and Po Tsai had begun to strategize on how they could defend their village; creating barriers and bunkers. She agreed it made sense to have the widows and children move to Huê, she also understood everyone was willing to fight for their homeland. Plus, it made sense to have as many able bodies to fight as possible.

As the sun was setting on a cool November evening, there was a knock at her bedroom door. It wasn't unusual to be disturbed at this hour.

"Enter," she called out. She was sitting at her table when Po Tsai opened the door and stepped in. He was carrying a white envelope and she recognized the wax seal.

"The messenger is back," he said without emotion handing her the unopened envelope. Mógū took a deep breath, he handed her the folded parchment as she exhaled. She opened it and read it out loud.

> *Zhèng de Guǎfù,*
>
> > *After much consideration and negotiations, I do believe we have reached a suitable arrangement that will benefit us all. To begin, let's start with the most difficult request; amnesty for all your men. Neither you nor them are welcome in China and will be treated as the criminals you are if you step foot in our great nation.*

"He called us criminals," she said looking up to Po Tsai with a smirk, then continued reading.

> > *That being said, we have reached an agreement with Anh of Dai Nam for your men and their families to be relocated to Huê where I understand there is property that has already been gifted to your crew. They may stay there and thrive until they die. The property is non-transferable and will be auctioned once there is no need to accommodate your people.*

Second, Cheung Po Tsai's reputation as a capable captain and warrior has preceded him. After much contemplation I can see how he would be a valuable asset in the Qīng Navy. If he is willing to swear allegiance to our flag and fight for the greater good of China, we can create an honorable officer's position for him. An exception for him to enter China at the harbor of where he would be serving would be prearranged. He would not be able to reside in China nor any of his offspring.

She looked up at Po Tsai and saw his mouth remained neutral but she could see the interest perk up in his eyes. She continued.

A suitable business has been acquired for you to own and operate in Macau. You will be granted amnesty from any prior wrongdoing you've committed in that country and left alone to run your business. As is the law, you will need to take a husband before the deed can be officially transferred into your name.

"Macau?" Mógū rolled her eyes. She glanced up to Po Tsai to gauge his reaction. To his credit, he stayed stoic.

You may keep one of the smaller junks in your fleet to continue the correspondence delivery system you have created. One. The junk shall be painted so it does not look like the vessels in your fleet. It must be easily recognizable and stay moored unless there are deliveries that need to take place.

In exchange for my generosity, you and your people will leave He On Kong and not return. This land has been conveyed to the British people and they will be settling upon it. Any and all of the treasure you have acquired shall be left where you stored it and will become the property of the Qīng Dynasty. You have until the end of the year to leave without bloodshed.

Furthermore; the British men you are holding hostage shall be returned alive immediately. This is non-negotiable and failure to adhere to this mandate will result in the above arbitration to be null and void.

A weight seemed to be lifted off her shoulders, she took in a deep breath and reread the letter to herself.

"You did it," Po Tsai said. Mógū could hear the admiration in his voice.

"It's not exactly what I—"

"It's a win," he said sternly with crossed arms and narrowed eyes, "what did you ask for you didn't get?"

"Macau?" she sighed.

"Youngyan doesn't want you in China. Nguyên Anh doesn't want you in Dai Nam." He held his hands out and shrugged. "You'll make more money in a port city like that than if you were inland. Think, woman."

He was right, she realized. She nodded and calculated how many more moons until the year of the Monkey. She would have Chūntáo and Wu Jun help prepare a harvest celebration and announce the plan to relocate everyone. The logistics were overwhelming but at least there was direction. When she woke this morning, she was envisioning a massive bloody battle with the Brits, training women in hand to hand combat to fight Youngyan's men but now...

"Looks like we're getting married." Mógū was lost in thought and Po Tsai's comment caught her off guard.

"Yeah," was all she could muster for an answer.

Chapter Forty-Six – A Different Kind of Wedding Day

Mógū told the delivery boy she would accept the terms outlined in the letter. From his jacket pocket, he withdrew two more wax sealed envelopes. One was red, one was white. He handed her the red envelope and tore the white one in half and returned it to his pocket. She tore it open and scanned the few lines.

A wise decision, Zhèng de Guǎfù. Join me and Emperor Nguyên Anh on the winter solstice in the capital city of Huê to work out the final details and sign the agreement.

"The honorable Youngyan requests I bring the prisoners back with me," the young man said standing at attention and avoiding eye contact with Mógū.

"I'm sure he does." Mógū laughed. "Tell him I'll bring them along in December. Assure him they are safe and well fed. Thank you, goodbye." The messenger opened his mouth. "No, don't speak," Mógū said quickly, "just leave. See you soon, the solstice is only a few weeks away. Bye, bye."

The news of relocating wasn't as well received as Mógū had hoped. Many of the older children as well as most men were ready and able to battle to protect their land. The women varied between wanting to stand their ground and a bigger desire to keep their families alive. Shouts and opinions were being cast at Mógū from every direction.

"If we stay and fight, it will be hard and many will die." Mógū stood and began speaking loudly so everyone could hear. "If we move, it will be hard but no one will die." She realized she got their attention with that comment, she pressed on, "Huê is a beautiful village with a lot of growth opportunities for many of you ladies. Seamstresses and quality teachers are needed in that area. And as for you men, if farming doesn't suit you, fish." A ripple of laughter moved through the crowd. She raised her glass in the air. "Thank you, every one of you. *Ganbei!* May our new life be as prosperous as the old." She downed the contents of her drink. Behind her Chūntáo began to clap.

Yīngshí yelled, "Ganbei!"

Many of the crowd cheered back as Mógū took her seat with Po Tsai, Chūntáo and the boys.

Plans were tentatively made and the junks were assigned leave dates and directions pending the final outcome of Mógū's meeting. Several of the junks would be traveling to Huê and a few to Saigon. As agreed, Mógū would be able to keep only one of the vessels. The others, after delivering her people safe and sound, would be sold at auction. Her plan was to give a few of the men enough coin to buy at least some of their junks. Certainly, they could find someone to do their bidding that wasn't on the government's list of known pirates. She would distribute some of the stashed wealth now to her people and give more in a year. By that time, they should be established in Dai Nam and not need additional assistance.

Mógū had also given her own junk some considerable thought. There was a green dye that was made with bamboo leaves. With Chūntáo's help they stained the ornate parts of the junk green. They took the red flags off and Chūntáo made new white sails with a green band that ran along the outside for added strength in high winds.

Mógū had stopped at Zhèng Yī's family shrine on several occasions. Most times she sat quietly, sometimes she talked to Zhèng Yī and told him her fears about the move and new brothel in Macau. Sometimes she could hear his laughter in her head, or feel his presence next to her. *It will all be fine*, he seemed to say.

One afternoon she heard the familiar gait of Po Tsai coming up behind her. Without looking over her shoulder she scooted to make room for him. He bowed respectfully at the shrine and sat next to her.

"I still miss him," she said. He nodded. "I'm angry sometimes I'm not fighting Youngyan to avenge his death."

"There was never proof he was behind—"

"You know it, I know it, do we need proof?" she answered with an unfamiliar whine in her voice. He reflexively put his arm around her and she leaned into him feeling his strength. "We should marry before we leave this place."

"We should do it now," he said and kissed her.

She watched as tears welled in Po Tsai's eyes. She kissed him back. "Yes, let's do it here. Now."

Peasant weddings were nothing more than sexual consummation, in fact, often they were pre-arranged and the brides were part of their family's own negotiations. There didn't need to be a ceremony, just sex.

As Po Tsai climaxed, he groaned in Mógū's ear, "I want a son too." Even though she hated the idea of another pregnancy it was only fair he had an heir. They lay together in front of the Zhèng family shrine lost in their own thoughts. Mógū's mind floated to another child. If she got pregnant with Po Tsai, she was sure it would be a girl. She didn't want to disappoint her new husband but she had a strong feeling about it. For the most part, they would be residing in different countries, living their own lives so perhaps it didn't much matter.

Chapter Forty-Seven – Parleys

Mógū had invited 250 guests to accompany her to Huê for the negotiations and celebration of the new amnesty deal with Youngyan and Anh. Her small junk could easily carry three hundred people. A sense of excitement was beginning to build in their village as the prospects of a new life in a new country settled in and with an added bonus of a trip to a city to celebrate, spirits were running high.

Emperor Anh was more than a bit surprised when her new green painted junk pulled in with the large number of people.

"We're all so happy," she said to the emperor as they disembarked, "it is a momentous occasion." She raised her cupped hand and twisted it back and forth in tiny waves as she walked down the gangplank. "Is that how George's people do it?" she asked Nguyên Anh as she marched past him to the waiting rickshaw.

That night there was much activity in the capital city. Mógū's people spent their money at the bars, food establishments, and gambling houses as well as booked every spare bed in the city.

The next day she and Po Tsai joined Anh and Youngyan in a large dining hall. Many women served hot coffee and small, sweet cakes. Mógū couldn't help but notice she was the only woman being served.

Youngyan had a small gong on the table in front of him. He tapped it lightly, the pure pitched noise reverberated through the large room.

"We have an important announcement to make before we begin these discussions of treaty," he announced. Mógū glanced at Po Tsai who looked as confused as she felt. "From today forward Nguyên Phuc Anh shall be forever known as the noble emperor Gia Long." He picked up the wooden hammer and hit the gong three times in a row. Anh stood and bowed as everyone clapped. Mógū went through the motions but didn't see anything to get too excited about. Names change.

The contract that had been written up had each of Mógū's requirements written out with additional clarifications. Youngyan's assistant read each specification and then it was asked if there were questions.

When they reviewed the stipulations of Po Tsai's agreement, Mógū spoke up, "You say that Po Tsai will have special access to China that the rest of us seeking amnesty will not have, correct?" Youngyan nodded. "What about his spouse or offspring?" The leaders shared a knowing look with a smirk. Mógū hadn't realized Po Tsai's liking of men was such common knowledge.

With a little laugh, Youngyan answered, "Of course we'll open our boarders to the wife and children of Cheung Po Tsai."

"Thank you," Po Tsai said with a forced grin. The reader continued to the next item, amnesty for everyone. There was an exchange about the Red Flag Fleet spreading out, as some wanted to settle far south in Saigon whereas the majority were happy to be in Huê even though the climate was much cooler. Since the properties had already been deeded to Mógū, it was only a matter of numbers.

"Once the fleet is auctioned, I think the money should go back to our men so they can reinvest it into your villages," Mógū suggested.

"Since you are taking their means of earning a living, they should be entitled to that money to start new land-based businesses."

"We cannot allow known pirates to have junks or ships or—"

"I completely understand," she interrupted, "which is why my men will need that money to make an honest living."

Youngyan nodded and Mógū motioned for the scribe to add the information to the contract.

Eventually they came to Mógū's stipulations and the business opportunity. "Will the brothel come with employees or will I need to provide my own girls?" she asked.

"Actually, at this time, it's a gambling house but prostitution is legal and you're welcome to staff it any way you see fit. Once you have a husband, we will be able to set in motion this requisite."

"I've already taken a husband," she said with authority and reveled in the confused looks that were passing between the men in the room. Po Tsai kept his eyes to the floor. "In fact, Emperor Long had inspired me today and I would like to officially change my name too." She indicated for Youngyan to hit the gong. He did so very lightly. "From today forward Zhèng de Guǎfù shall be forever known as Madam Cheung Po Tsai." Mógū gave Youngyan a huge smile knowing he had already agreed to a special pass into China for Po Tsai's spouse.

"Is this true?" Nguyên Anh questioned Po Tsai.

"Mógū isn't one to make stuff up," he answered.

To be fair, she didn't really have any desire to visit mainland China but she never knew what could come up. It was better to have a backup plan if she needed to travel to China. She stood as Gia Long had done and bowed then gave Youngyan a puzzled look and motioned for him to hit the gong.

Mógū sat at the bar in her lucrative gambling house and brothel. It was the ten-year anniversary of Chūntáo's death. So much had changed in the last decade. Mógū poured another shot of rice wine into the small glass.

"Miss you, little sister," she mumbled as she drank down the bitter booze. Chūntáo had died from the second wave of cholera pandemic, the last of her allies to leave her. "I've outlived everyone I've ever loved," she said to herself as she banged the glass on the bar top.

"What'd you say, mama?" Mógū's daughter asked, "you doing fine?"

Táozi (Peach) was her youngest child but even she had grown into a middle-aged woman. It was she who ran the business now, Mógū was nothing more than a constant honorary guest, part of the furniture. The gambling house with a small brothel upstairs proved to be enough income for her to live comfortably and raise Po Tsai's and her children.

During these past decades, Mógū was restless and at times bored, but she lived in financial security which was more than most could say. Chūntáo had been her constant companion after Cheung Po Tsai set sail with the Qing Dynasty.

She had gotten pregnant on the night she and Po Tsai sealed their marriage on one of their last nights on He On Kong Island. It was the son he had been desiring even though the pregnancy was so different than her other two she was certain he was a daughter. They named him Yú Lín.

A few years later, she had gotten pregnant again on one of their rare trysts and Táozi was born nine moons later. She was the apple of Mógū's eye. It was different to have a girl. Between her and Chūntáo, Táozi was indulged and spoiled.

"Spoiled good, like grapes," Chūntáo was fond of saying as she raised her glass of ruby red wine. The memory made Mógū smile.

The move to Macau in the spring of 1811 was difficult. Mógū had a hard time staying put in one place and running a business. She craved the sea, the fight, the treasure. Chūntáo kept her entertained. She was more than a friend; she was a partner. She helped Mógū run her company and raise all four of her children.

The two of them had made little dolls resembling the working girls they employed just like on the flower boats. Táozi had wanted one too so they made one for her even though she would never be that kind of working girl.

They continued the gambling commerce because it brought in good money with little to no effort on their part. They had hired pretty girls to oversee the dice pits, and if there was any cheating, there were always a few young men who were more than happy to escort the offender outside for a lesson in gambling etiquette taught by their hard fists. The years peeled off quicker than either of them could have imagined.

Yīngshí was the spitting image of Zhèng Yī. He had grown to become the captain of his own explorer ship. He would sail through the Macau port every other year to keep Mógū and Chūntáo updated on his life. Those overnight stays were always welcomed and celebrated. By the time he was thirty he had three children, two girls and a son, who lived in Thailand with Yīngshí's wife.

Xióngshí had become a scholar and taught secondary school in Da Nang. He was the most animated of her children. As a storyteller and teacher, he was able to work anywhere he lived. Xióngshí had helped his mother with the sales of the riches that had been stashed in the caves of Huê. Once the families of the Red Flag Fleet had become independent in the new Vietnam, the rest of the treasure had stayed hidden until long after Cheung Po Tsai had been killed. Then it had surfaced in bits to be sold, the money going to him or one of his siblings or on occasion back to Mógū.

Mógū's third son had walked in his father's footsteps and joined the Chinese Navy as soon as he was old enough. The boy had been serious from his infancy and stepped into a military career with ease. It had seemed to Mógū, Yú Lín and Táozi were much more difficult to raise even though Chūntáo said they were easier.

"Harder because you're actually around," she had teased Mógū, "you somewhat skipped out on the first two." Chūntáo had been right, raising children was every bit as challenging as marauding the South Seas.

Cheung Po Tsai had been gone twenty-two years now. Mógū had always believed the Dynasty had Po Tsai killed, assassinated. The story they had fed her when he died never felt right. There were too many holes, too many inconsistencies. Cheung Po Tsai had been piloting his own ship for most of his life and the accident that supposedly killed him was nothing more than an amateur's mistake. She believed that Youngyan had some sort of revenge he waited patiently to dish out to her. In her heart, the Qīng Dynasty murdered both her husbands.

She drank down another shot of the rice wine. Where had the time gone? She had grown old too quick and now here she was, a successful business owner in Macau with four grown children and two dead spouses. She picked up the opium pipe that sat on the bar and added some of the sticky stuff from a wax paper with a tiny knife then held it over a candle.

"Wish you were here," she said even though she wasn't sure who she wished was there. She filled her lungs and let it out with a sigh. A bright light flashed as the front door opened. It caught her attention and she turned to look. The entrance faced north. It was night. What could have reflected to make that kind of intense light?

A slender man had entered her establishment and motioned a greeting to Táozi and walked towards Mógū. He looked familiar. She bent over the candle and took another hit from the opium pipe. When she looked up Zhèng Yī was sitting on the barstool next to her. Her first thought was it was Yīngshí, until he spoke.

"Hello, my dear."

A smile pulled across her face. "Hey."

"Ready to get out of here?" He looked so young, so handsome. Of course, she was ready to go. They could sail the world together now. Suddenly Mógū couldn't speak, her tongue betrayed her, it felt as if her mouth and brain were no longer connected. She swallowed and nodded.

Zhèng Yī held out his hand and she stood and stepped away from the bar. All of her aches and pains were gone. She felt young and healthy. As they walked out of the building arm in arm she glanced over her shoulder and saw the shell of an old woman slumped forward, her head turned sideways, eyes and mouth open.

Táozi was gently shaking her. "Mama, mama? Are you alright?"

Author's Note

Prior to the Covid-19 pandemic, my favorite two things to do were travel and write. I've discovered a new story idea in every city I've ever been to; Hong Kong was no exception. Raymond, my husband, and I spent New Year's '17-'18 on Lantau Island where we were invited to a swanky dinner party. My third book, *Trials & Tribulations of Modesty Greene* was getting ready to be released that March. Naturally, I gravitated to the other author in the room, Simon, who was also a pilot for Cathay Pacific Airlines. He explained he wrote nonfiction, specifically instruction manuals and 'how-to" books. I gave him the run down on my three novels.

"If I could write fiction," he said to me, "I'd write a book about Ching Shih."

I had no idea who he was talking about but as he told me the story of what little was known about her life, I couldn't help but be intrigued. Her story was something legends were made of; brothel boats, plundering, murder, and a bizarre love triangle. I was dumbfounded no one had written a book about her life. The wildest imaginations couldn't have come up with a better story. Ray and I did some research and explored old town Macau where Ching Shih had her brothel and went to a few museums that highlighted her virtually unknown life. It was a fantastic trip with many wonderful memories. The vacation ended, we went back to the US. My new book came out, my day job took over the majority of my time, and life went on.

I have a personal goal to write a book a year for the rest of my life, so when 2019 rolled around, I needed a new book idea and began researching Ching Shih. What I discovered was there wasn't much to discover. There was not much info about her and if not for Richard Glasspoole, I'm not sure there would have been any historical recount of her life.

During this time, I learned Ching Shih means 'widow of Ching' but the spelling is the Romanized version of the Cantonese name Richard Glasspoole used. This amazing woman was so much more than the wife of Zhèng Yi, I couldn't help but create my own name for her, Mógū.

When it was time to create the audio book, my new narrator pointed out some glaring mistakes I had made throughout the book combining Mandarin and Cantonese. Another round of edits ensued to create some consistency. At this point, I had already fallen in love with the main characters and their names; the majority of them being Mandarin where they might have been Cantonese if the book was one hundred percent historically accurate. As the author, I found myself pulling the "it's fiction" card and leaving Po Tsai's name with the Cantonese spelling and pronunciation but updating Mógū's sons' and brother's names to the Mandarin versions. The rest was checked and rechecked to the best of my ability.

Most importantly, this note is to thank you for supporting me in my passion for writing. It's what I love to do and that's what life should be about, doing what you love.

Sincerely,
DW

About the Author

D. W. Plato has been writing for as long as she can remember. She once said, "Give me thirty minutes in a hostel, hotel, or hospital, and I can walk out with a novel idea." With her ability to easily make friends combined with her gift of gab and an overactive imagination, this statement isn't a stretch.

Check out D.W.'s other great books. Her premier novel, *The Sinners' Club* (2016), atheist boy meets Mormon girl, a little dogma romance with LGBT side stories. *Glue* (2017) when one woman leaves her husband for a better life she finds herself going down a tunnel of sex and drug addiction. *Trials and Tribulations of Modesty Greene, a fictional novel about Harriet Tubman's historical legacy* (2018) a pre-civil war story about one woman's enslavement experience and it's generational repercussions. *In the Interim* (2019) a story that explores the ideals of family, friendship and murder.

Made in the USA
Las Vegas, NV
16 May 2022

48980491R00140